THE BEAST

& THE

BEAUTY

NIKKI STEELE

ABOUT THIS BOOK

This is a **Bad Boy Erotic Romance**. It contains violence, drug references, and strong, explicit, smoking hot sex scenes.

It is a re-imagining of the Beauty & the Beast fairytale, but it is **NOT** something for under 18s

You can find all of Nikki Steele's books at
www.nightvisionbooks.com/books

DEDICATION

To KS. The love of my life, the inspiration for my dreams, the editor of my madness, the fire under my feet. I've done a lot of silly things in my time. Asking you to marry me wasn't one of them.

NIKKI STEELE

1: BELLA

If I bought enough dresses, I'd be sure to miss my date.

Good. I'd heard the man was a buffoon. It was why, though the sun was falling in the South American sky and Papa had wanted me back at the embassy hours ago, I was still shopping at the local markets.

I'd reached the edge, where the market bordered the local prison, when I heard the shout from behind me. I cocked my head, deciphering it. Though my brown hair and pale white skin marked me instantly as a foreigner, I spoke Spanish because I'd grown up in Southern California. *Get out of the way?*

I spun to see a huge man dressed in rags pushing his way past a table piled high with chilies in the distance. Seven-feet tall and all muscle, he towered over the people and market stalls around him. He yelled again, pushing past bright yellow bananas and piles of beautiful silk, stumbling in his sprint as he swerved to avoid a woman and baby. Far behind him, several people yelled and pushed after him in chase. The giant had the look of someone hunted—an escaped felon.

He drew closer, barreling through a stall. Cherries flew in every direction. His face was pulled back in a snarl. I looked across the garbage filled strip behind me to the huge grey walls, 40 feet high, that towered nearby. If he was escaping, why was he running *toward* the prison?

When I turned back, people had cleared a path. He sprinted along it.

Directly toward me.

"Get out of the way!" His eyes locked on me, the only person left in his path.

But I didn't obey the command. I couldn't. I stood like a deer on a deserted road as a truck barreled toward it. Like the truck's headlights, that intense stare had me frozen to the spot.

God had granted the man a physique to match his height. Huge, tattoo covered forearms rippled with muscle as he motioned me from his path. "Get out of the way!"

Slabs of broad chest peeked through rips in his shirt. His hard face was close enough now to see a massive scar that ran the length of one cheek. He was beautiful, in that way that only something truly terrifying can be. His broken nose creased as he scowled.

"Get out of the…"

The huge, terrifying, *beautiful* man pulled up, stumbling to a stop. "…way," he finished softly, his eyes going wide. The anger drained out of his eyes' slate gray.

"What's your name, girl," he said, his voice husky yet soft.

My lips moved, but no words came out. I knew I should be scared. Around us, stall keepers were hurriedly packing up their wares. But despite his size and obvious strength, those eyes said he wouldn't hurt me.

He glanced over his shoulder. His pursuers were getting close—four men that wore pissed expressions and prison guard uniforms. My breath left me in a whoosh. *I was right. He was an escaped prisoner.*

He leaned close. I'd thought his scar marred only his cheek. But it ran the length of his face, curving along his powerful jawline and disappearing into his hair. It moved as he spoke. "What's your name?" he asked again.

Yells came from behind him, and still I couldn't answer. He glanced over his shoulder once more. Something gold glittered in his tattooed fingers. Powerful, callused hands reached out to grip mine gently.

I should move. Run. But I couldn't. He stared into my eyes a moment, before pushing something into my palms.

Rough hands grabbed him. His muscles trembled and his knees buckled, but even with four men pulling on him he did not yield. Gray eyes stared at me as guards wrapped arms around his waist and neck. Finally, only after it was clear it was his decision, not theirs, he allowed them to pull him to the dirt.

"Bella," I tried to whisper. *"My name is Bella."* But my mouth was dry, no words came out.

Those eyes never left mine as the guards cuffed his wrists before him. It took all four to haul him to his feet. Then they spun him, and marched out into the 100 foot, garbage filled expanse that separated the market from the towering grey wall on the other side.

The state prison.

Its outer wall must have been 40 feet high. Beyond it, individual buildings peeked out at haphazard intervals like turrets from within the compound grounds. If the prison was a castle—and it looked like it with its ramshackle towers and massive gate—the strip they were marching the prisoner across was its dirty, junk filled moat.

I drew a deep breath, ignoring the pungent aroma of rotten fruit. He'd asked my name, this beast of a man with such kind eyes. At the very least, I could give that to him. "My name! It's-"

At the sound of my voice, the stranger turned to look at me. A guard raised a truncheon at his sudden movement. It came cracking down on the prisoner's head.

I screamed as they beat him—hard violent punches and kicks that he wore silently, his head bowed, collapsing slowly to his knees in the junk filled earth. "He's not fighting!"

They ignored me. If anything their beatings, in the long shadow of the castle, grew harder. The muscled man's fingers clenched earth, but he didn't fight back. I ran towards him, but then stopped. What could I do? I wasn't strong like the man. I didn't have any authority, like the guards. And I hated confrontation—it was the whole reason I was at the markets, not back telling my father the ambassador, 'No.'

They continued to kick and punch him—much more than any normal man could take. I called out, terrified to come closer, but they wouldn't stop.

Eventually, a kick to his ribs elicited a moan. The guards laughed, and kicked him again.

At the sound of his voice—that voice which had been so soft, but was now in so much pain—I leapt forward, finding my courage at last. I grabbed the first raised wrist I found. "Don't hurt him, please."

The owner backhanded me casually. "Fuck off. Don't stick your nose where it doesn't belong."

I stumbled away, hand going to my mouth. One guard turned from the prisoner to shove me. I cried out as my feet left the ground, then again when I hit the red dirt.

A growl rose from the stranger. It was the sound of a predator—a snarl that hung in the air, building in tempo as his muscles bunched. Then he roared, the sound sending birds flying up from the wasteland with a screech.

Too quick to register, he was on his feet, swinging his shoulders like wrecking balls and his head like a sledgehammer. His legs kicked out. His arms swung. The three guards still around him went down in a heap.

The giant stepped forward. His tattered shirt ripped as the last guard clutched at it but was pushed flying away. The massive, muscled man stood panting above me, then bent down. "Are you okay?" he asked. He extended his hands.

His body was covered in tattoos. On his right shoulder, a shattered clock, the numbers running backwards. Script in a foreign language covered a scar on his chest. Everywhere else, animals of every shape and size snarled in beautiful, horrific detail.

I nodded mutely, transfixed.

He rocked to the side, grunting, as the guards picked themselves up from the ground, shaking their heads to clear them, then leapt upon his back. But he didn't falter until I was safely on my feet.

"Thank you," I whispered. I was so overwhelmed I couldn't say anything else.

In a concerted effort, the guards tried to drag him away from me. He planted his feet, hunching his shoulders to stay where he was. Still our eyes were locked.

"No. Thank you," he said. His head tilted. "It's been a long time since someone tried to protect me." Then his shoulders relaxed, and he allowed himself to be yanked away.

Free from me, the guards beat him again. His mission accomplished, the man didn't fight back.

"No!" I screamed. "He's not resisting!"

The man held my eyes through it all, until he was lifted to his feet and dragged across the wasteland towards the prison once more. Then, incongruously, he gave a bloody smile, as if to say it had all been worth it.

I stood there another heated moment, the market at my back painfully still. And then the people regrouped and there was noise—people haggling, hawkers crying their wares. It was just another afternoon at the market, after all. They must be used to this.

I wasn't, though. Not the beatings. Not that man who'd been so gentle despite his size.

Aching fingers unfurled to discover a heavy gold Rolex watch in my hand. I frowned, lips moving wordlessly as I attempted without success to make sense of the gift. I'd seen a dozen of these already in the market. If I had to guess, I'd say this one, too, was fake.

2: RIO

I paced the small cell, fighting against the rage threatening to consume me. I called it *the Red*, for what it did to my vision, though it was also a fitting description for the stains not yet washed from my knuckles. The Red had come upon me in the markets, when the guards pushed over that woman. I still suffered the after effects now — short, sharp bursts of anger that left me blinded.

I'd been so close — that damn watch in my hand. If only I hadn't been distracted. If only I hadn't let my eyes linger on that woman's face, or fall to the shape of her breasts beneath that gauzy shirt, I'd still have it. My anger flared, the last remnants of that rage in the markets... but then it strangely fell.

Her skin was the most beautiful shade of white, so different from my own Latino tan. That thick mass of dark hair falling down her back and those wide and innocent eyes had stopped me in my tracks.

Beneath that gaze, I'd frozen. Even now, the memory made me pause, unsure of my place in society, but

13

convinced it was at the opposite end to hers. It was as if comets had smashed together in the heavens, raining down sparks of *something* upon me. Something that made the air shiver and the heavens tremble with an emotion other than my rage.

It had been a long time since I'd felt like that. As though the world contained something that was precious, and needed protecting. Like I wasn't worthy, but if I tried hard enough, I might gain redemption.

It was funny how all those thoughts could flash through my mind in the space it took for our eyes to lock. That moment when our hands had touched had been worth the beatings and the loss of the watch.

I punched the cell wall, oblivious to the pain in my knuckles. What did it matter? I was in here, she was out there, and I was unlikely to come across her path again. A swell of anger rose in my throat.

"*El Lobo.*" The rap of a riot stick on metal bars interrupted my pacing.

"What?" I snarled, spinning to face the two guards watching me from the corridor. I recognized the older one through the spaced metal bars—a henchman for the prison warden. The other had the scent of someone new—his back was too straight, and his eyes too wide.

I leapt at the bars, rattling them, and my lips curled as the new man stepped back.

The older guard chuckled. "Be careful around him," he told his fresh-faced compadre. "Like his wolf namesake, his bite is worse than his bark."

The younger guard scowled. I scowled right back, still pissed about my beating, and losing that watch. It took time for the new guards to learn the rules here—they thought that a uniform and a weapon made them a king who could do as they pleased.

The older ones knew better—they were kings of the wall only. Inside, a different set of people ruled—the gangs, who swarmed the courtyard like hyenas. The dealers who swarmed the weak like jackals. And *el Lobo*. The Beast with his thousand tattoos, one for every man that had challenged him and lost.

You might trap a beast, but you didn't poke it, in case one day it got out of its cage.

The new guard tried to approach me, but the older one held him back. "What happened? You were supposed to be out and in without anyone being the wiser."

My fingers unclenched, then clenched again. I'd been poked hard, today, when I was put back in my cage. "I was doing just fine, until your assholes jumped me. They were just supposed to follow—make sure I didn't run."

"And *you* were supposed to get coca leaves from the market."

I clenched my hands, fighting my anger, but didn't respond. It was ironic that in el Castillo, the biggest drug dealers of all were the guards. But there was no better production facility than a walled compound where labor was free and worked for life. They'd been using me to buy their ingredients in bulk, without getting seen.

"Fuck you." Remnants of the Red forced the words from my mouth before I could help it—a primal link between my heart and my lips that bypassed my brain entirely. "I'm not your dog on a leash. Say what you want, but we're done here. Find a new man to do your bidding."

The new guard moved closer, a flush creeping across his face. He rapped my cage with his baton. "You know who the boss is around here, don't you, *el Lobo*?"

His tag said his name was Ramirez. A tattoo of a tear decorated his right cheekbone. He'd been in a gang, as a youth, to get that tattoo. *A tear for a life taken.*

My fingers flexed. *I hated the gangs.* Past or present, it didn't matter. "Nice tattoo."

Ramirez's hand went to his cheek, unsure how to take the compliment.

I beckoned him closer. "I know what it means."

He leaned forward. "Do you now? Then you'll know not to fuck with-"

My hand snapped through the bar as he came within reach. The sound of his head connecting with metal as I seized his hair and *yanked* brought a vicious smile to my face.

He fell to one knee, dazed, as the bars vibrated in dull resonance.

"I don't bother with tattooing tears anymore," I said. "I've lost count."

Ramirez stood, stepping back from the door, blood pouring from his nose. "Open the door," he told the other guard. "I'm going to kill him."

His companion chuckled, shaking his head. "You deserved what you got. I told you before we walked in here that this one was dangerous."

"He won't be dangerous when he's dead!"

I growled. The Red made me equal parts stupid and strong. "Just try it."

"Watch it, el Lobo," the older guard cautioned. He pulled his companion back. The man was fumbling for his gun. He put a hand on it to stop him. "There are people we can kill, and there are people we can't. Killing this one would cause a riot."

"He'll pay for this shit," Ramirez said. But his gun slid back in its holster. He stalked away from us both.

The older one waited a moment longer. "Useful doesn't mean invincible," he cautioned. "Even kings can be toppled. Take care, lest *el Rosario* comes knocking on your door." Then he turned and followed his younger counterpart toward the exit.

He left me alone with my thoughts. The momentary enjoyment of seeing that new weasel bleed faded, and my thoughts returned once again to the events in the market. The Warden would be angry. I should have done what I'd been sent out there to do first, and picked up what I'd needed after.

Strangely though, that wasn't what distressed me most. More than the beatings I'd received, more than the punishment to come, the thought that flitted time and time again through my mind as I resumed my pacing, was that I'd never got her name.

I knew her face—it smiled at me each time I closed my eyes. I knew her body, with its soft curves and pale white skin. I'd known her touch, if only for a moment. But these were all disparate things—fragments with nothing to bind them together. I'd asked her name, and she'd not given it. And somehow that, above all else, was what pained me most.

3: BELLA

It was only when I arrived home, panting, that I realized I'd completely forgotten about my date. I'd spent the entire time thinking about that huge man in the market. When our eyes had locked, all of civilization had faded away. There'd been something... primal about him. Huge and beastly, with his arms and neck covered in ink. His snarl as he rose would have put a bear to shame.

But that look in his eyes—that had been human. And when he'd asked my name... I shivered, wrapping my arms around myself. That had made me feel human, too. The date only entered my mind when I found a man with a long black ponytail standing on my door in a cloud of cheap perfume.

He looked like a 1980's advertising executive—blue eyes, square jaw, tight red shirt and a grin made of Pearl Drops and Vaseline. *Great.*

Papa came out to see us off. "Here are the happy couple!" he said, shaking my date's hand furiously. "Bella, this is Gateau. *Like the cake, ha ha.*" My father's bushy white eyebrows jumped up and down like excited caterpillars as he spoke. "Gateau was such a help when I first came here. He has all sorts of government connections even though he's from America, too."

Papa had moved to South America as an Ambassador several years ago. I was visiting because I suspected that he was lonely here, though he'd never say it over the phone. He worked long hours. I only saw him in the evenings. Apparently, Gateau was Papa's solution to me not getting lonely while I was where, too.

I rolled my eyes. "It's just coffee, Papa." I didn't need a man in my life, no matter my father's best intentions. "We'll only be gone five minutes."

Gateau cleared his throat. "Nonsense!" his voice was deep, and just a little too loud. "We're going to dinner, my treat."

Great.

Father turned to me, giving me a hug as if I was about to embark on a grand adventure. Then he stood back to look at me. "My beautiful flower," he said fondly. His gaze softened, and he pulled a tiny box from his pocket. "These earrings were your mothers. I'd like you to have them."

I bit my lip, my throat tight. "Oh, Papa." When I opened the box, two tiny, delicate gold rosebuds lay glittering on a white pillow.

He looked away as I put them on. "You're like she was in so many ways," he said softly, a hand brushing at the corner of one eye.

Then he clapped his hands together, forcing a smile. "Now go on you two. Have fun!"

***

Despite my father's wishes and my mother's jewelry, dinner with Gateau was just as horrible as I'd imagined. From the moment we'd walked out of the compound, all he'd talked about was himself, and how much better he was than 'the natives.'

By the time we sat down, I hadn't said a word and was already out of things to say. He was a stuffed poodle—perfectly groomed, horribly coiffed, and utterly convinced of his superiority.

"You know, my colleagues are fine, for Latinos, but they can't beat my American education."

"She's a local. She probably stole it."

"You have such beautiful white *skin."*

Gateau regaled me with tales of vacations in distant lands—South Africa, Venezuela, India—any place, it occurred to me, that a white man might go to feel better about himself. The stories assaulted me like a tide that never ceased its assent upon the shore. Eventually, I ordered a bottle of wine.

The only exciting moment came when Gateau mentioned, in passing conversation, that two backpackers had done a tour of the local prison, last week.

"Really," I asked, putting down a vegetable I'd been stabbing over and over with a fork, imagining it was Gateau's face.

He nodded. "I have some small influence in the prison. I like to keep a tab on events. I got them immediately kicked out, of course."

"Oh." A million things had just run through my mind—me, doing a prison tour. That rugged stranger, in irons. His gratitude, when I gave him back his watch. "I wonder if…"

For the first time since dinner had started, it seemed that Gateau could read my mind. "Fat chance," he burst out laughing, "that place is now locked down tight." He chortled. Little bits of chicken sprayed from his lips to land upon my plate. "I mean, I could get in—all the guards know me. But someone on their own wouldn't stand a chance."

A tour of the prison though! My heart fluttered at the thought of meeting that stranger with the jagged scar and wild eyes again. Suddenly I couldn't wait to get through the night.

4: BELLA

The guard pulled me into the shadow of the huge, imposing prison. "Gateau sent you?" he asked.

I swallowed, my throat dry, then nodded. "Of course," I lied. "He said you did prison tours, and to mention his name at the door."

The guard had watched me, eyes narrowed, as I picked my way toward him across the junk filled strip that separated the prison from the markets, skirt hem lifted to avoid the mud. No doubt he'd been wondering what the hell a *gringa* like me was doing in this place. I'd spent the entire time wondering the same.

Last night, I hadn't been able to stop thinking about the stranger. *Those eyes.* Steel gray, and so intense I'd stopped breathing when they met mine. Those calloused hands, gripping me so softly as they'd pulled me from the street. I'd pleasured myself to that memory, after dinner with Gateau. That feeling of contentment, as I lay in imagined arms, had stayed with me as I drifted off to sleep.

When I'd woken this morning, a feeling of destiny had settled upon me, as if my entire life might turn and take a new direction, if I could only help it on its way. I fiddled with the gold watch I now wore on my wrist, unsure what I was doing, knowing only that if I stopped to think too hard about it, that feeling would go away.

"You can help me, can't you? I need to give something back to someone." I'd visit his cell. Give him the watch. Stand with iron bars between us, or maybe a glass partition, and get the chance to tell him my name.

"Be quick then, before anyone sees. I'll swipe you through into the prison proper." A security card flashed. A heavy door opened. We stepped into a tiny white room with a long white table.

"What about my guide?" I hissed as we strode to a second door on the other side.

He paused, eyes narrowed. "Gateau sent you. Didn't he arrange a guide as well?" His hand hovered above the security terminal. "Tell me now if you're lying, little girl. This won't be good for you if you are."

I gave him my best *white-girl-privilege* look, inspired by Gateau. "Just do your job, or face the consequences."

He rolled his eyes. "Yep, Gateau sent you." His fingers tapped out a quick staccato on the keypad, then he escorted me to a final, heavyset door. He frowned at me, as if still unsure of the right thing to do, but then set his teeth and punched in a code. We walked into a long, narrow guardhouse on the other side. A lone guard manned it. He looked at us curiously, and then looked away with disinterest.

The guardhouse stretched inwards all the way from the first, massive gates that I'd seen on the outside to a second set of gates that were in front of us now. Between them, a third pair of gates which were twice as thick stood open. *Three rings of security, but...*

"Why are the big doors open?" I asked my guard.

"I'm not your tour guide. Are you going to do this or not?" he asked, as I paused at the door.

I gave him the white-girl-privilege look that had worked so well from before.

He sighed. "All deliveries come through the main gate," he said as if reciting a policy word for word. Perhaps he was. "In the event of a riot or national emergency, the blast doors"—he gestured toward the large middle gate— "are closed and the prison locked down." He eyed me. "A time delay is set when they are locked. Neither the gates or these doors can be opened again without an override from the Warden. Are you sure you want to do this?"

I sniffed. "I'm not afraid of staying a few more minutes in here."

"Who said they'd only be locked for a few minutes? A lot can happen to a pretty white girl who doesn't know what she's doing. The people in here aren't human any more. They're animals, and they'll rip you apart if you give them the chance... or you're lying about why you've come here…"

I swallowed. "So, I just find a guard in the prison when I want to get out?"

He laughed. "You really don't know what you're doing, do you?"

I crossed my arms. "You've got my money. And Gateau is a close friend. Don't try and back out now."

He shook his head. "You deserve everything you're about to get, as far as I'm concerned. But here's something for free. There *are* no guards in the prison."

I stilled. "No guards?"

"Why do you think we're all gathered here behind two layers of reinforced bullet proof glass? There's 700 of them and only 36 of us. We man the walls and occasionally throw in food. You'll need to come back here to get out, so don't go too far inside."

I swallowed again.

He grinned maliciously, showing yellowed teeth. "Think of el Castillo like a village where all the occupants are murderers and rapists. They look after themselves—if they don't try to get out, we don't try to go in."

"You… ah, you're sure I can't get you to come with me?"

He smiled, moving closer. "Not on your life. But if you've suddenly changed your mind, I can think of other things we could do to pass the time." He leered, and the scent of old onions washed over me from his breath. "A pretty young thing like you would be a pleasant change to the prison whores."

I pulled away from him. "Not on your life."

His smile disappeared. He grabbed me by the arm. "Then stop wasting my time." He held out his hands.

"What? I already gave you money."

"No phones allowed on the inside."

I drew my cellphone out of my pocket. "This?"

"No. The one in your shoe."

He snatched at it, but I pulled it away. My cell phone was my life! It had all my friend's details. It had Facebook. It had pictures of my mother. "Do I get it back?"

His hands gestured impatiently. He leered. "Does it have naked photos?"

I pulled a face. *The creep!* "Of course not."

"Then I think you're going to be safe."

The other guard looked up and snickered. He had a small tattoo on his cheekbone. It jumped like a corpse in a noose when he laughed.

I handed my phone over doubtfully.

"My shift ends in one hour—be back here by then or you'll have to stay overnight. *With the murderers and rapists.*"

I shook him off—he was trying to scare me, but I wouldn't let him. I'd made it this far and I wasn't going to turn around now. "I'll see you in an hour."

He shrugged. "Suit yourself." Then he walked to the final door, keying in a combination to swing it open with a gesture. *"Be our guest."*

I took one step forward, then another, willing myself not to hesitate. I straightened my shoulders. *And walked into the unknown.*

The door clanged closed behind me, echoing the muted laughter of the guards through thick plate glass at my back. I stumbled to a stop.

The prison was dirtier than I had thought it would be, and… not that much like a prison at all. Dust hung heavy in the air, catching the light that reflected from the broken shards of glass in the prison blocks that towered four and five stories above.

They ringed three sides of the courtyard that I now stood in—a ramshackle collection of buildings that stretched off into the distance and must once have been clean and habitable, but now reminded me of a slum; the roofing was rusted, the walls were crumbling, all the windows had been smashed out. I'd expected the concrete gray of a neat, ordered cell block. Instead, I was greeted with the dull browns and yellows of a land that time had forgotten.

But the people… looked normal. That took me by surprise. I didn't know what I'd been expecting, after the guard's words—every second person sharpening their teeth with daggers, perhaps? But there were men and women, boys and girls scattered around the edges of the courtyard. Even the odd dog scurrying around. This was a community—albeit one where every single person had presumably done something bad.

I stepped tentatively forward, noting the laundry that flapped from the balconies—bright colors occasionally, but for the most part dirty rags and tattered clothes. I'd come here to find the stranger. I wasn't going to do that standing with my back to a bulletproof door.

Dirt puffed in a low cloud as I inched across the courtyard. The entire space was the size of a small playing field, ringed with decaying stone arches that led into the slums. I picked an arch at random, squared my shoulders and strode toward it, wondering how on earth I was going to find the stranger—I wouldn't be able to go too far inside, or I would get lost.

Halfway across the yard, I noticed a group of three men loitering against the wall of the arch I was approaching. They rose and began walking toward me, fanning out across the courtyard. From a distance, they each had shaved heads and wore dirty football jackets. As they got closer, I saw malice in their bloodshot eyes. I stepped to the side, uneager to be in their way. They changed direction. I stepped to the side again. They adjusted course once more.

Their leader, a dirty man with a strut like a rooster, wiped his nose with his sleeve and laughed. I swallowed. When I looked behind me, the guard who had let me in was pointing toward them and grinning, like I was about to get what I deserved.

5: RIO

Mateo tugged on my arm, pulling me along dirty corridors I'd never been in before. The small boy—barely seven years old, wanted to show me his new favorite hiding place. I tried not to think about why he wanted to hide.

He motioned at what looked like a storage closet. Like most rooms in this hellhole, the door of this one was useless. Someone had punched holes through it in the past and it hung off its hinges like a crack whore clinging to a lamppost.

I pushed past it, stepping into the storage closet and made a show of looking around. It was long and deep, with buckets stored in one corner and old towels arrayed upon a shelf. Perhaps I could steal a few for my gym.

"Well done!" I said, signing with my hands as I spoke. I wasn't as fast as Mateo, but I'd been trying to pick it up. He rolled his eyes, pointing at a jumble of boxes as high as the roof, at the far end. We walked toward it in silence.

Mateo never spoke when his hearing aids didn't work. His mother thought it was psychological. I tended to agree.

It was why I'd been so angry at losing that watch. It had been a tacky, fake Rolex, and worth so little to the vendor that I'd bought it for the pennies I'd held in my hand. But like so many things in life, it was what was inside, not on the surface, that counted.

None of that mattered now. The watch was as lost to me as the woman—a memory to haunt me at night; a chance at a better life failed.

Mateo beckoned me to the boxes, oblivious to my thoughts. I forced a smile on my face for his benefit. "Yes, very good," I said, signing. "A great place for hide and seek. You could crawl up into one of the boxes…"

I paused. The boxes *looked* like they lined the back wall, but there was a space behind it. And in that space, was a door. I pushed against it. It swung open on its hinges, fully functional.

I frowned as my eyes adjusted to the low light. At some stage in the past, the storage room had been divided into two. The outer door had been smashed in. The inner, hidden by the boxes, still survived.

Doors in el Castillo were valuable. I could count the number of intact ones on one hand, not including the metal gates leading to the outside. "A good place to hide indeed," I signed. "A great spot for hide and seek." I raised an eyebrow. "Maybe we could even practice your signals here, one on either side of the door?"

He pulled a face. I'd been teaching the boy Morse Code, just like he'd been teaching me sign language. He couldn't hear the noise, but he could feel the vibrations, with his hand up to a door or pipe. In the absence of sound, it might be another thing to keep his senses stimulated.

The skepticism that presented itself upon his face made me laugh. So far, he hadn't been too receptive to my ideas. But my humor faltered as I studied the room. It was small and bare, with no windows. A single light bulb hung from the roof. It didn't work when I tried to turn it on.

I bent down before the little boy. "Why are you showing me this?" *If someone was hurting him...* the Red blurred my vision at the thought.

But the child grinned, chest puffed out like the basilisk lizards that sometimes made their way into the gym. His hands moved in a series of quick flashes. *'Do you like it?'*

I nodded. "I do."

He took my hand and placed it upon a box, then tapped out his response in Morse Code upon the cardboard. *'I knew you would.'* He turned away, like that was enough of an explanation.

The child was so bright, and he was only seven! I'd have to make more time for him, if I could.

My eyes flicked to the working door once more. Maybe I'd also come back later, when Mateo got sick of his new playhouse, to take it down. If he wouldn't use it for practice, I could put it on the room he shared with his mother. Perhaps it would encourage her to stay home more.

We were walking back to my district, hand in hand, when a figure charged down the hallway toward us. "Ay, el Lobo!" Lumen, though barely out of his teens, was my second in command. His small frame vibrated with urgency as he stopped to hop from foot to foot before me. His thin face contorted as he ran fingers through his wild hair. "I've been looking for you everywhere!"

Immediately, I tensed. "What's wrong?"

"There's something happening outside. In the courtyard. I think you need to see."

I pushed Mateo into Lumen's hands. Lumen didn't come to me with idle requests, and the look on his face said this was urgent. "Look after him. Get him home. I'll get there as quick as I can."

6: BELLA

They surrounded me like coyotes circling a lamb. "What brings you out here, pretty?"

The man that spoke was ugly; his shaved head a brown, speckled egg with sunken eyes that glittered beneath thick, black eyebrows. I twisted to keep him in my sights as he took off his football jacket and threw it to a companion. He wore a dirty white wife beater underneath, and his bare arms revealed a tattoo of a razor dripping three drops of blood on one side; multiple needle marks on the other.

"I don't want any trouble," I said nervously.

He snickered, then flashed me a blackened grin. "Too late for that."

I looked around wildly, only then wondering if there was a reason people lined the outside of the courtyard, but avoided the middle. "I... ah, Gateau sent me," I said desperately. I didn't know if it would work, but it had let me in, magically, at the gate. Maybe it would get me out, now.

"Excellent," he purred. "I knew he'd come through in the end."

One of the gang leaned in, snatching at my dress. I tugged it hurriedly away, causing them to cackle again. Another flashed in from the other side. This time the fabric tore at one shoulder, and I screamed. No one came to help—if anything, the people on the outskirts of the courtyard scurried quickly away.

I edged back toward the guardhouse, stopping when I thumped into the hard, thin body of the leader, who had circled behind. His arms snaked around me, that tattoo on one side and those needle marks on the other.

"Where are you going, *chiquita*? There's no need to rush. Why don't you tell me about those pieces you have?"

The leather skinned man spun me to face him. I froze, a mouse in the gaze of a snake's dark, evil eyes. *Pieces?* At my look of confusion, one of the man's hands fingered his earlobe. *My mother's jewelry.*

I slid the gold rosebuds free of my lobes. "Here," I said, dropping them into his hand. Father would understand. "Take them." His fingers were calloused. When they closed, the nails were embedded with dirt.

"That, too," the man said without preamble, gesturing to the watch on my wrist.

It was the one the stranger had pressed into my hands the day before. I'd brushed the dirt from it and cleaned the face. I'd brought it with me just in case-

A dirty hand leapt forward, yanking the watch from my wrist. I cried out in pain as my arm twisted. "Please, no!"

When he'd undone it, he pushed me away. For a moment, I thought I might be free to go. Then a second set of hands grabbed me. "Now, we'll need that dress," my captor whispered.

A chill settled over me as I realized what he was implying. My mouth opened in a scream, but a third set of hands clamped over it. "Let's go for a walk somewhere less public. I think you'll rather enjoy what we have in mind."

The guardhouse was my only hope. But the men there just looked back at me and waved. This, it seemed, was the lesson that spoiled rich girls deserved.

Teeth bared in a snarl, I bit down on the hand covering my mouth and was rewarded with a yelp. The injured hand slapped me hard across the face. "I was going to make this easy. But now, now you're going to…"

His eyes widened as he saw something behind me. "Oh, shi-"

He didn't finish as a shape rushed past me, a huge wall of tattooed muscle that slammed into him, knocking him off his feet. He flew backwards with a cry. The wall of muscle turned, and then the stranger from the market scowled down at me.

"You shouldn't be here," he growled, eyes flicking to the other two skinheads.

"She's ours," my assailants said, pushing me behind them to face off against the hulking brute. "We saw her first."

The stranger shook his shaggy mane. "You're wrong. Leave her, before you get hurt."

One of the skinheads moved, and then all three were rushing him, surrounding him; coyotes giving up their lamb to take down a lion. He beat one back with a massive clenched fist, but another leapt upon his back, arms locking around his neck. Fear lanced through me as I watched a second gang member grab him, then the third stumble to his feet and do the same. It was the scene from the market happening all over again.

This time, though, there were no handcuffs to handicap the stranger. He heaved his arms together and two shaved heads collided before his massive chest. The skinhead clinging to his back was flipped over his head and into the dust. Animal tattoos moved upon the stranger like wild beasts as his fists lashed out. He was a whirlwind of muscle that towered over the smaller dogs nipping at his heels.

Their leader scrabbled back, blood dripping from his nose to spatter his razor tattoo with new drops. "Mercy!" he cried. "In the name of the Agreement!"

The stranger reached down and grabbed the man by his collar, lifting him clear off the ground. "Why should I care about our agreement, Diego? You were about to rape this woman."

"It was common ground! We didn't know she was yours!"

He threw the man backwards into his friends. "Get out of here," he snarled. "This one is mine. Don't let it happen again."

All three ran as fast as their injured bodies could take them, hobbling until they had disappeared through the far arches and out of sight.

They were gone just a few moments, not even long enough for me to turn to my rescuer, when people started to trickle into the courtyard once again. Had they been clinging to the darkness to avoid the gang? And if so, what did it say that they came out now?

My rescuer growled, still looking toward where his assailants had run. When he'd moved, it had been like an animal. Even now, standing still, he was a predator—his muscles coiled beneath his clothing.

A memory of last night came rushing back to me, unbidden. In my fantasy, I'd imagined his hands upon my body, doing to me what those men had wanted to take by force. My face burned, partly in shame, partly in gratitude. I approached him cautiously.

"Thank you, I-"

"Don't," he snapped, turning on me. The rage he'd shown earlier had left his body, but not his voice. "You were a fool to come here."

"I... I came to see you," I said, taken aback by the words. My hands went to the watch at my wrist, but of course it was gone. *God. Did he even remember me?* After all I'd been through—I was such a fool. My eyes started to burn. "I was at the markets yesterday," I whispered.

His eyes closed. His shoulders lost some of their tension. "I remember," he said. "Why did you come here?"

I searched desperately for something to say, as around us, people filled the silence with talk and laughter. Between us, there wasn't a sound. How could I say that I'd dreamed about him? How could I tell him why I was here, when I didn't know myself? "You gave me your watch," I said eventually.

"Do you still have it?"

I shook my head. "Was it important?"

His eyes closed again, briefly. "It doesn't matter, now."

"You saved my life."

Gray wolf eyes studied me, their expression unreadable. "They wouldn't have killed you."

"They would have made me wish they had."

He drew a breath but paused, and then nodded. "You're dangerous."

"Me?" I asked, eyes wide. "I don't understand."

"Exactly. There's a balance here—a precarious one that you couldn't possibly understand—and you upset it." Shadowed eyes flickered toward the guardhouse. "I shouldn't have done what I did. There will be consequences."

Horror and anger curdled together in my stomach. "You would have let me be raped?"

He snarled, fists clenching, his rage back in an instant. "No, goddammit. *But I should have!*"

The slap of my palm against his face rang across the square. "How dare you." Around us, the chattering stopped.

He didn't move, even as a red welt spread across his jaw and my hand began to sting.

"Two hundred and thirty-seven," he said, staring into the distance. Eyes like storm clouds then focused on me. "That's the number of people under my care. That I protect from the Razors. That I feed and shelter in my quadrant." His fists clenched. "The Razors will come for me after what I've done. If they kill me, that's two hundred and thirty-seven more people they'll have to prey upon."

My hands went to my mouth. "I'm sorry. I didn't know."

He turned and strode toward the guardhouse. "Two hundred and thirty-seven," he said angrily, as if he hadn't heard me. He gestured for me to follow. "And you won't be number two hundred and thirty-eight."

100 feet from the guardhouse, I paused. "I'm sorry," I said again, watching the muscles of his back ripple beneath his ripped shirt. I could see the shadowed lines of those tattoos I'd seen yesterday upon his skin. "I really am. And I'm grateful, for what you did."

Turning to face me, those steely eyes softened. The man I'd met yesterday was back. "I... I'm angry, sometimes. It's the only way I know how to survive."

He was apologizing too, in his own way. He rubbed at his scar. "I can't afford weakness. Too many people depend on me here."

I took his hand in mine. It was rough, the fingers broad and callused. "You saved me," I said, raising my other hand to trace the scar on his jawline - just like he had done himself moments before. "I think you're strong."

His lips parted, just the slightest of movements. But then his jaw set, and his hand slid from my grasp. The man I'd known yesterday disappeared. "If you stay any longer, it will get me killed."

He turned, shoulders stiff, and began to walk away. After a moment's hesitation, I spun and did the same, walking back toward the guardhouse. My eyes burned. I don't know what I'd expected, but it wasn't... this. Each step toward safety felt like a step in the wrong direction. As though I was fleeing from something more important than I could possibly realize.

A guard stood before the gatehouse door, arms crossed, as I wiped at one cheek. "Sir, I think I'm ready to go, now."

It wasn't the guard who'd let me in, though I thought I recognized him from earlier. His eyes flicked from me to the stranger, who was still walking slowly away, his back stiff. "You know that man, do you?" he asked, fingering a bruise that ran under one eye. He had a faded tattoo of a teardrop on his right cheek. The bruise had turned it purple.

"He saved me," I said simply. "I came to visit him, but now he doesn't want me anywhere close."

His eyes narrowed. "Why."

"He says that my presence will get him killed."

The guard's fingers fell from the keypad that would let me inside. "Sorry, sweet cheeks, no can do."

"What?" I asked, confused.

"I can't let you inside. Enrique has gone home, and he's the only one that can vouch for you. I wouldn't be doing my job if I just let any old person walk out these gates."

Apprehension twisted my insides. "No, listen, you saw me inside, before. I have to leave-"

"Not anymore." He laughed, and pushed me away. "You're going to have to stay a little while longer."

I rushed toward him, but he stepped back and pulled his gun. I froze.

"I get twitchy, when I get rushed. Don't do it again," he said.

"Please."

"Your contract was with Enrique, not me. It's not my fault if I'm just following orders."

"But you know me! You know I'm a visitor!"

His eyes flicked to the stranger. "I don't know what you're talking about."

"I can pay!"

He sneered. "With what? Come back tomorrow. Enrique said you had an hour. You blew it, now you'll have to face the consequences."

He backed away as I stood helplessly before him. As he keyed in the entry code to the guard quarters, he called out to the stranger walking way. "Hey, *el Lobo!*"

The stranger stopped, then turned.

"I told you I'd get you. Enjoy looking after the princess in here."

His laugh cut off abruptly as the door slammed shut behind him. I hammered on the thick glass, horrified, as I realized that I was trapped in el Castillo for the night.

7: RIO

I'd taken three strides toward her before I forced myself to stop. "Two hundred and thirty-seven." The whisper hung in the dusty air that surrounded me. I had more than a quarter of the prison to look after and constant jackals biting at my heels. I couldn't afford to take her on.

Let her hammer on the door. She'd give it up soon enough. Someone in the courtyard would take pity on her. And if not, many a newcomer had spent their first night in a corner, tucked out of the wind. She had her health and her sanity. She had a free pass, at least until the Razors worked up more courage. Hadn't I given her enough?

Three strides. I couldn't afford any more. Not the hundred strides that I wanted to make; to rush to her and wipe the tears from her cheeks. Three strides, and 237 people.

With every pound of her fist against glass, I told myself that I should turn and walk away. But when she turned, spotting me standing in the center of the courtyard, I knew it was too late.

Pleasure tingled in my heart as she approached. I forced it down, doing my best to remain angry. "You're dangerous."

"He wouldn't let me through."

"You'll be the death of me." I folded my arms across my chest.

"What am I going to do? I shouldn't be here."

My eyebrow shot up at her statement. "You think any of us deserve this hellhole?"

"Help me. Please. Just until tomorrow."

I closed my eyes, trying to find the strength to tell her to find a corner—to curl up against the wind and wait out the night with hunger gnawing at her belly like a thousand inmates had done before. Like I had done, on my first night.

I turned on my heel. "Come with me." I'd feed her before she found her cold corner. I shouldn't even do that, and I was so angry at myself for even offering it that I didn't wait to see if she would follow.

I strode across the courtyard, the look on my face clearing a path more efficiently than my height or physical bulk ever could. Soon, I heard the patter of footsteps behind me.

"Where are we going?"

"The tower."

"What's your name?"

"You don't need to know."

I was being purposely obtuse, and I knew it. But I was breaking every rule by helping her out. She should be grateful I'd answered her at all.

By the time we'd walked through stone arches three quarters of the way down the courtyard, she'd fallen blessedly silent. Our footsteps echoed on the cold, shadowed concrete of a corridor, and then fell away as we entered sunshine once more.

"Where are we?" the woman, now beside me, asked as she looked around herself, eyes wide.

I smiled. "The Gym," I said softly. I'd built it by hand, weight by painstaking weight, when I first came to el Castillo. The demand for it among a predominately male population, particularly one that survived on brawn and testosterone, had been the initial basis for my power.

Though the gym was pitiful by outside standards, it was a paradise within. In one area, iron bars with concrete blocks mounted on either end served as weights. The iron had been pulled from old cells—none of the rooms in the main prison still held their bars—and the concrete, I'd chipped by hand from an old nearby wall. Exposed roof rafters served as chin up bars in another area. Hand weights were either filled jugs of sand, or assorted lumps of iron.

I stole a glance at the woman beside me, with her beautiful skin, pretty dress and hands that had never known a day's hard labor. And suddenly, doubt filled me.

What did this ramshackle collection of junk look like to her? Outside gymnasiums must be electronic wonderlands. Membership in one, I'd heard, cost more than I'd earn in a lifetime inside. "It may not look like much," I said defensively, "but in a society where you start with nothing, this is years of work."

I waited for her to contradict me, more nervous than I had a right to be. What did I care if she thought this was junk? Tomorrow, she'd be free to leave, and I'd never see her again.

She walked to the weights, with their roughhewn forms. Her fingers ran along edges that I'd lovingly ground down by hand.

"It's… clever," she said eventually, her eyes filled with surprise. "I would never have thought this was even possible. You're so resourceful."

My back straightened slightly, before I caught myself. "Yes, well," I said gruffly. "You do what you have to when you don't have any other choice."

I motioned her through the area, past curtained off cells and makeshift front doors. Evening was fast approaching, and with little power in the prison, and therefore few lights, people were starting to settle in for the night.

The other gangs and leaders charged rent for their beds and floor space. I opened mine up to anyone with just a few simple rules—no stealing, no drugs, no murder. And my word was law. Gym 'membership' from gangbangers keen to increase their muscle mass paid for the bribes to guards and food for all.

My stomach growled as we neared the eatery, an area also within my domain. A few select cafes, serving food purchased from guards, lined the walkway. Their windows were boarded closed; the haphazard tables and chairs stacked against the walls. Pickings had been slim, recently. Word had it that the Warden was keen to make more money out of us, but none of us were rich enough to pay.

The eatery, when we arrived, was crowded. Almost all 700 inmates ate here over the course of each morning and evening, regardless of class, society, or gang affiliation. Razor skinheads ate in one corner, the few white supremacists ate in another. The drug addled, the prostitutes and transvestites; everyone ate their fill.

I maintained a strict *neutral ground* policy in this area. It was self-policing—those who started fights went hungry for the next seven days, and quickly learned their lesson.

For the most part, the meals were the same day in and day out—pitiful rations given from a central station and served by a prisoner allocated cook. For the last two years, the cook had been Lumen. He might be young, but before he arrived, he'd worked in an industrial kitchen.

He slopped lumpy gray sludge into bowls. Rumor had it that he bribed the guards in exchange for secret herbs and spices. I knew the falsehood of it, but the buzz that he also filled the gruel out with pigeon and rat had more than an element of truth. If we didn't, there wouldn't be enough to go round. We did what we could do survive.

My station meant I could skip the line, and my mouth watered as the scent of stewed meat filled my nostrils. *Rat—my favorite.* As far as I was concerned, it just added valuable protein.

"I see you found her," Lumen said, looking past my shoulder. She was cowed behind me, the stares of several hundred prisoners on our backs.

I nodded, then shook my head as he offered me a bowl. I never ate in public. Though the Eatery was neutral ground, I would eat later tonight, when I returned to my room.

"Do I feed her?" he asked.

I hesitated. Whilst it had been a long time since I'd had a meal on the outside, I was pretty sure that rat hadn't suddenly become a delicacy. "Do you have anything special?"

"I have some bananas I've been saving."

"I'll owe you, if I can take two."

"You do enough here, *Rio*. If you want them, they're yours."

I took the proffered bunch—spotted yellow and brown like a leopard's coat—and we moved to a quiet corner. "Here," I said, offering the food to her.

She took it hesitantly. "That stew smelled good. Could I have some of that?"

I wanted to laugh. I'd just offered her fresh fruit—actual fruit! —worth more than what everyone else was eating combined, but she wanted the rat. "That's not for you," I said, clearing my throat.

"What, is it prisoners only, or something?" she asked, peeling a banana.

"Something like that," I said, eyeing it as she ate it. Something about the way her lips closed over the top, nibbling at it, made me swallow. I tried to convince myself that it was because I hadn't eaten fresh fruit in a month.

She slid more of the banana into her mouth, lips wrapping around it. I turned away, on the pretense of inspecting the Eatery, adjusting my stance slightly to relieve a tightness that had sprung into my pants. "If you come back tomorrow morning, I'll arrange with the cook for more fruit before you go."

Silence from behind me. I turned, to see the woman staring at me with wide eyes, the banana halfway to her mouth. She quickly swallowed. "You're not…" She started again. "What will I do tonight?"

"Sleep, if you can."

"Where?"

I shrugged uncomfortably, ignoring a tug at my heart when I thought of her huddled in a corner, alone. "This area is the safest. You can find a wall, or a corner, and then-"

I broke off, at the look in her eyes. "I'm sorry!" I snapped. I'd known she would assume I'd organize her accommodation, but there was none to go around. "This isn't one of your fancy hotels on the outside. I can't just snap my fingers and have someone prepare a room for you. It's a prison!" I didn't need to be someone's knight in shining armor. That was the Rio of the past. Here I was *el Lobo.* And I didn't have time for things like that. For people like her.

A flush of color swept up her cheeks, startlingly beautiful on her clear skin. It chased away the pallor that had come with discovering she was locked in the prison for the night.

"If I could maybe just stay with you until morning," she began. "I could sleep in the corner, like you said. It's just… you're the only person here I feel safe with. I promise I won't be in the way…" she drifted off, a look of pleading in her eyes.

I took a step toward her, letting my size and bulk tower over her. Perhaps intimidating her would give me the space I needed.

But my move was a mistake. She smelled sweet, like fresh air and sunshine. How long had it been since I'd smelled fabric softener, and real perfume? It made me want to pull her closer; inhale her more deeply.

I kept my hands firmly at my side. "What makes you think you'd be any safer with me than out in a hall?" I growled. There was more truth in my words than I liked to admit. I itched to lay my hands on her, to slide them up over her body and run them along the same curves I couldn't tear my eyes away from now.

"Please." Her eyes flitted to mine. She bit down on her lip.

I lifted a hand to her cheek, before I could stop myself. It moved slowly as her eyes widened, her body taut. She was tensed, though perhaps not to run. I drew it down her face, mimicking the mark I couldn't escape on my own. "You don't know me at all."

The statement hung between us, but she didn't back down. Or flinch away from my touch.

After a long moment, I dropped my hand. "Fine," I said, exasperated. "You can stay with me tonight."

8: BELLA

The sun had set, and darkness seeped into every corner of the prison. I followed the stranger—the guard had called him *el Lobo*, yet the cook had called him *Rio*—through dark twisting corridors and up multiple flights of stairs, higher and higher, until the stairwell ended at a metal door. He pulled a key from his pocket, inserting and twisting it with a metallic clink.

His quarters were simple. *Sparse.* A lone cot in the corner, bolted to the wall. A small table, and a barrel filled with water.

Two doors led to a small balcony. When I stepped outside, I had an uninterrupted view of the stars. Below, the courtyard lay in darkness. The balcony was slightly higher than the wall surrounding el Castillo. City lights shone tantalizingly close, just out of reach.

Something thumped against the wall behind me. My rescuer had thrown a tattered, thin blanket into a corner. "Here," he said gruffly. "You take the bed."

"I'm happy to-"

"I insist."

I hesitated, but the evening had brought with it a chill. The cot was a hard board covered by a thin layer of foam, but the sheet was clean and the bed large enough for me to stretch out fully. It was a million times better than the cold, hard floor. I eased myself between the cheap cotton sheets. I didn't take off my clothes.

"Where will you sleep?" I asked softly.

Part of me feared he would say 'beside me'. Part of me feared he wouldn't.

His eyes flickered over my body, hidden beneath the sheets. Then his shoulders set, and he looked instead to the corner he had already claimed. "I'll be fine. I'm used to the cold here. You're not."

"Thank you," I said meekly.

He nodded, exiting to the balcony and leaving me alone with my thoughts.

This high above the prison, everything was silent. I lay back, but soon found I couldn't sleep. *Night in el Castillo.* I'd wanted to know what it was like inside. Now I did.

At home my bed was soft and pink and fluffy. I knew I shouldn't complain—I could be on the floor, or worse, sleeping outside, under the stars, but that didn't stop my back from aching. I didn't want to think about how I might have spent the hours until morning had this man not taken me in. *Had he not rescued me from the skinheads.*

I wriggled onto my side, propping my hand under my head like a pillow. I could see his silhouette against the dark blue of the night sky. Arms braced against the railing, looking over a city he could see but never touch. The stars lit his dark, shaggy locks, outlining him in a halo as he stared out into the darkness.

For a long moment, he peered into the night. Then, in beams of light from a moon rising slowly above the horizon, he tugged his shirt over his head. My breathing stilled as he undressed—his back arching, his arms above his head. I drank in his broad, heavily muscled back.

Tattoos draped his body like silks—animals that I had seen on his arms and neck extending across newly revealed, sculpted flesh. I should look away, but I couldn't. I'd dreamed about the body beneath his clothes. The reality was better than any memory that I'd pleasured myself to last night.

Shirt held in one hand, he looked out over the city beyond the walls for several moments more before turning to glance into our shared room.

Now, I closed my eyes, fear that I might be seen watching making me pretend to be asleep. I heard him pause in the doorway briefly, then pad softly to the far corner.

Rustling, then. The clink of a belt.

I cracked my eyes just the smallest fraction to see his pants folded on the table beside his head, and a flash of boxers before he climbed beneath his blanket. The animals traced upon his arms and shoulders rippled, settling down for the night with him in the darkness.

I shifted slightly, warmth appearing between my legs that hadn't been there before he stepped out upon the balcony. It must be a chill from the open door, making the rest of my body cold.

Yes. That was it.

I wrapped my arms around my chest. This was the man who had rescued me. Who, despite knowing he shouldn't, had fought for my honor just hours before he gave up his bed.

If I was cold here, how must he feel on the stone floor?

A rustle of cotton that surprised us both—my hand, shooting out from beneath the covers. "Please. You'll get a chill."

His eyes glinted in the moonlight. "I've endured worse." His voice was low, but sound carried in the stone building.

I shook my head. I owed it to this man to give him at least the comfort of his own bed, tonight. "Stay with me. I trust you."

He hesitated, but then stood, unfurling from his blanket, a bear from his cave. He padded across the floor in his boxers. I swallowed as the wall of muscle approached, my eyes upon his, fighting not to let them drift lower.

He climbed in beside me. There was enough room for us both, barely, if I lay with my shoulder touching the wall, and his stayed on the far other side. His body was warm, beside me. His breathing was a soft rhythm next to mine.

A shiver slid through me. I wasn't cold anymore. Far from it. I swallowed, only just now realizing that I'd gone from sleeping alone, to watching a man undress, and then inviting him to lay beside me in the blink of an eye. What must he read into that? What did I want him to read?

But he didn't touch me. He was on his back, one hand stacked behind his head. I stiffened, trying hard not to even breathe, for fear and want of my body touching him first.

"I don't bite, you know," he said finally.

I let his statement hang a moment before turning toward him to find a more comfortable position, still careful not to touch him. My skirt was tangled around my legs. I slipped my hand under the sheet to free it.

And found my hand accidentally brushing his leg as well. I drew it back quickly, but not before a hot thrill at what I'd done shot through my body. *I'd touched him!* And I wasn't sure what exactly it was that I'd touched.

"Your name?" he asked, his words tight. They emerged thick and low in his throat like a growl.

"Bella," I said. "I heard you were called Rio."

"That is true. My mother always said I was unstoppable, like the rivers she named me after."

"And el Lobo?" I asked, my breath catching. In Spanish, el Lobo meant *the Wolf*.

He shrugged, beside me. "I am the beast of el Castillo."

"I don't think you're a beast," I said, my heart pounding in my chest.

"I am. You just haven't seen it yet."

I swallowed. They were just words. They shouldn't have been making me want things I couldn't have.

He'd said I hadn't seen the beast. But I had, hadn't I? In the ferocious way he'd defended me? What other animal instincts was I yet to awaken?

I owed everything to this man. My life. My body...

My hand crept toward him. I owed this man so much. But that wasn't why I wanted to feel his skin. *His body*. Was there softness beneath that hard muscle? Was there softness beneath those hard eyes?

My fingers touched his skin, just below his ribs. I broke out in shivers, that flame growing hotter between my legs.

But he pulled his hand from behind his head, stilling my fingers. "You shouldn't," he said, his voice strained.

"I know," I said. He smelled like smoke and metal. I didn't remove my hand.

He turned toward me slightly. "You said you trusted me."

I moved my hand out from under his and toward his face. I traced the scar on his jaw, the bristle on his cheeks tantalizing on my palm. "I do. You saved my life."

His words were now a ragged gasp. "But I don't know if I can trust myself."

I pressed closer to him, the curves of my body settling against his hard chest. This was the man who I'd dreamed about, who fate had brought me to lie beside. I owed him so much—my life, and my body. I knew how I wanted to repay that debt.

"Show me the beast," I whispered.

It was the last invitation he needed.

In a single movement, he pulled me toward him, his mouth crashing upon mine. His body leaned into me, heavy. It invoked something primal in response. I reveled in the crush of his lips, the urgency of his hands. In his tongue as it slid against mine. I lost myself in the kiss. I ran my fingers through his hair as he tugged at my blouse.

"Rio," I whispered, testing the name on my tongue. He pulled the cotton above my head. I moaned at the feeling of flesh on flesh.

His hand slid down, his lips still busy. They cupped my bra, and I arched beneath him. I didn't know what I was doing. I wasn't this sort of girl. But the beast had awakened something in me. I couldn't stop the direction in which we were heading. The heat at my hips was a raging fire.

He growled as his fingers reached behind my back. A click, then he was ripping my bra from my body with his teeth. I sighed as my hands went to his head, holding him to my chest. Then gasped as his lips found one of my nipples, adding further heat to the inferno between my legs.

I bit my lip then, to keep from making any sound. But it was soon an impossible task. I cried out as the sharp pull of his mouth upon me, hot and demanding, sent my fingers clutching through his hair.

His hands moved lower. *Oh God. This was happening.*

Fingers pulled at my skirt. My own followed eagerly, tugging at his shorts. I'd been so enraptured of his lips upon me. So in love with his teeth nipping gently at my breasts. But now, my attention was on the hardness of him, at my hips, huge and pressing into me.

I needed to see the beast. To feel it. To tame it.

As he lifted my skirt I pulled down his shorts, releasing him. My hand grasped his length. *A beast indeed.*

He growled at my caress. I thrilled at the heat against my palm.

"Bella." His hand pulled urgently at my skirt once more, lifting it, until his fingers slid beneath my underwear. They found the very core of me.

I cried out, then pressed my mouth into his shoulder to cry again as his fingers began gentle circles, his rough calloused hands a tantalizing delight. My own palm sought to return the favor, but it moved only in haphazard strokes. I struggled to concentrate as he moved upon me, to share with him the pleasure he released in me. I rocked against him, eager for his touch.

It was just as I had imagined it would be. His hands were gentle but insistent, coaxing me until I was a trembling mess of nerves and pleasure.

My palm left him, forcing his own hands away as well. I scrabbled at my panties, dragging them down my legs. I needed more than this. I needed him in me—to feel the beast when I shuddered and trembled.

His mouth came down on mine again as I settled him between my thighs.

He paused to run his thumb over my lip. Events began to catch up with me then, in the pause. *What was I doing?* Did I even know this man? I knew only that he was more animal than human. That he had fought for me like a beast.

Then he pressed into me. Hard. Driving all the way to the hilt. I gasped.

And all thought fled my mind again.

He was so big! He filled me completely; driving that warmth he'd generated away to replace it with a raging fire. I thought I'd known pleasure, before. But I knew better now. This… this wild, unrestrained joy. It was like I'd only just now been made whole. His shoulders were muscled places of worship. They caught the calls to God that issued from my mouth.

I met each thrust with one of my own until I was caught up in the sensation of him sliding in and out, the hard planes of his body against my soft ones. He growled deep in his throat, and then sunk his lips to my breasts once more.

"Rio!" I was close now. His name was no longer strange upon my lips. Trembling and eager, desperate for the end that was fast approaching, I called his name again.

My fingers raked down his back, then clutched his hair. I pulled his lips to mine, kissing him, tasting him, making him *feel* my urgency in the hard crush of my mouth.

His motions grew faster as his lips returned my urgency; his stubble scratching at my chin and cheeks. We moved in unison, our sharp, hard bursts of breath tandem signs of excitement. Those wolf eyes were wild. But then mine must be too. We were two animals upon a tangled land of sheets.

He swelled, and drove into me one final time. I cried out as my hips clenched and my body shook. When he released inside me, I trembled and shook all over again.

He stilled, panting; his face pressed into the hollow of my shoulder. The aftershocks were still coursing through us, and for a long moment he remained where he was, buried inside of me, his hands still tangled in my hair.

It took a long time before I had the strength to open my eyes. Rio's remained closed, his fingers trailing the line of my jaw as we rolled apart. I stared up at the ceiling, trapped in prison, lying beside an inmate, and wondered what I'd done.

9: RIO

For the first time since I could remember, I wasn't torn from sleep by the nightmares that usually haunted my dreams. It had been a long time since I'd had a woman in my bed. Longer still that I had enjoyed the sensation of her falling asleep in my arms, her whole body slowly relaxing as I stroked her hair.

I stroked her hair again now, trailing my fingers through the long strands, breathing deep as she slept nestled into my chest. Her shampoo was scented—jasmine, perhaps. If anything, it made her naked form even more feminine.

I gritted my teeth when I caught myself smiling. *What the hell had I gotten myself into?* This woman was an outsider. She didn't belong.

Worse, I'd crossed the Razors to fight for her. I'd won, but their defeat would leave them sore. To parade her before their noses, as I'd done at dinner, was like throwing matches at a room full of dynamite. Sooner or later, if you did it long enough, one would strike and set the world alight.

I should be rid of her before that happened. I should turn her out, for the good of 237 other people who relied upon me for food, and shelter, and life.

I tried to force my fingers to still. To push her away. But I couldn't do it. And so I lay in my bed, wrapped up in a stranger I had no business touching, in a place where she had no business being, wondering if suddenly, I'd committed to 238.

It would have been in both of our best interests to have avoided last night. But there was no going back, I knew that already. I didn't want to kick her out. I wanted to have her again—to feel her trembling beneath my fingers and sighing against my skin. And more than that, I wanted to protect her. In prison, they called me el Lobo. Last night, for the first time since I'd arrived in this God-forsaken place, she'd made me feel human again.

She blinked owlishly when she awoke, as if trying to place exactly where she was and how she'd gotten there.

Then she stiffened.

"Oh God." Her face turned pink and she scrambled from the bed, pulling the sheet with her to protect her modesty. When it revealed my naked form underneath, the pink turned even darker, racing across her neck and chest with rapid heat. She spun, rushing to pick up clothing which lay dotted around the room.

"You must think I'm a…" She left the last word unsaid, scrabbling to do up her bra. "I don't usually do this sort of thing, you know…"

I growled. *Like I did?* The day I'd been betrayed and arrived here, I'd sworn I'd never let another use me again. Last night, I'd risked everything, only to be repaid with a look of horror on this woman's face. Rage began to boil and bubble in my chest. She was using me, just like the last. She didn't care. I was nothing more than a bed and a brief diversion.

No, that thinking wasn't right. I bit back my first response, fighting to think logically. I was so used to just snapping, so used to letting my anger override rational thought.

She was scared, that was all. Embarrassed. She wasn't the sort of woman who did this. It had nothing to do with me.

Last night, Bella had made me feel human. The vestiges of it remained now—I used it to push the rage back. To think things through.

My reward was her taking the silence for contempt.

"Whatever," she snapped. "Think what you want. I know I'm… I'm not your usual kind of woman anyway—I don't charge."

Again, I took a deep breath. She wasn't used to saying those kinds of things. She tripped over the words, trying to choose just the right things to say. Looking for a way to hurt me, I supposed.

I stayed silent. We wouldn't see each other again. We were from two different worlds.

237. Her words would only make it easier.

"Forget it," she snapped, wrapping her arms around her middle. "I'll be on my way and you can get back to whatever other women you have lying around here for your personal use."

"Perfect," I muttered. My first words. And then she was gone. And that was probably for the best as well.

10: BELLA

I refused to cry about it. Or even think about crying about it.

It wasn't like I knew him, or was invested in him. He was just someone I had slept with. And even if it had been shockingly good, it had been nothing more than sex.

Just one night. Something that shouldn't have even happened. And however gentle I'd thought he might be, whatever kind of values I might have imagined he had, I'd obviously been deluding myself. He was just a man—no, not even that. A prison inmate, a killer or worse. I should never have entertained the thought of him as a lover.

There was only one positive element within this whole mess—there'd be no running into him accidentally on the outside. No having to deal with the embarrassment or shame. I could walk out of prison, never see him again, and try to forget this had ever happened. As hard as that would be.

Something about forgetting Rio bothered me, but I pushed it away. We were from two different worlds. It could never work out. His assumption that last night had meant nothing was for the best.

I began to walk down the stairs, trailing my hands along the stone walls on one side to keep my balance. Down the stairs, through the arch, and out into the courtyard-

Where I was abruptly knocked to my knees in the dirt.

I looked up with wide eyes, then ducked as a fist swung over my head. It wasn't aimed at me, rather, at a man on the other side. He went down beside me and I stared at him numbly for several seconds as his head bounced upon the dirt.

What? What was...

Fingers grabbed at my body, shoving me as I tried to get back up. I was suddenly eye level with several sets of legs and boots once more. I tried to catch my breath and get my feet under me at the same time—and failed miserably as another body landed beside me, this one spurting blood.

I screamed, the noise tearing from my throat as fear knotted like a ball in my stomach. I scrambled to my feet, only to be pushed back over again. I'd stepped into a brawl, and it was quickly spreading; more and more players rushing in from every side of the prison; a turf war, the combatants distinguishable only by the tattoos upon their skin.

A homemade knife—little more than sharpened steel wrapped in tape—glinted in the hands of a youth to my right, then buried itself in the side of a man with a broken nose on my left. He went down with a gurgle, clutching at me. I screamed again, stepping backward, until rough hands seized my shoulders. I spun to find bloodshot eyes looking at me, and a tongue that licked across yellowed stumps of teeth. "What have we here? El Lobo's lady. Diego told me about you." His friends on either side grinned. "What a shame you got hurt in all the confusion…"

I drew my breath for one final, hopeless scream, but it was drowned by a roar of anger behind me.

Bloodshot eyes and yellowed teeth disappeared in a mist of bone and blood and my assailant flew to the ground. His friends on either side disappeared next—a blur of tattooed flesh striking left and right to clear a path around me. The breath that I'd drawn in to scream let itself out in a rush. *Rio.* Rio was here, and as he flashed a look at me—a look that said to stick close—I knew he'd come through once more.

The turf war was getting larger. The courtyard that had been so empty the day before was now a mass of heaving, screaming, crying, sobbing, and bloody bodies. Some lay on the ground, others trampled those below, fighting for position. Rio stood, the eye of the storm, even two gangs jacked up on juice and lusting for blood weren't crazy enough to mess with *The Wolf.*

Over everything—the screaming, the bloodied gurgles and cries—a loud, piercing siren started. It echoed off the walls, punching at my ears. I looked wildly for the guards, my heart leaping, but instead saw only violence. What had that first guard said? *There's 36 of us and 700 of them. In the event of a riot the prison is locked down.* I swallowed, finally realizing what that meant as I heard the echo of the prison's riot doors slam closed. *The guards had left, locked the gate, and would only re-enter when the violence was over.*

A man screamed for help. I looked over to the entrance where a group of guards hammered on the gate. *They'd been locked inside—too slow to get out.* They went down under a swarm of prisoners and the flash of a bloody knife.

Rio continued to savagely attack anyone that strayed too close, the circle getting smaller as both sides became emboldened. Someone reached for me from behind. Rio's fist hammered against their temple. Another person grabbed at my skirt from the side. His boot cracked into their kneecap. But not even Rio could stop the inevitable press of people. His hand wrapped around my arm and lifted me from the ground, hauling me like I weighed nothing more than a feather, before pushing me toward a deserted patch by a wall.

I pressed myself flat, shying away from the tsunami of people, and searching wildly for an exit. But I didn't move. I couldn't leave Rio while he was in the middle of that circle of angry men.

I forgot to breathe, watching the bodies slam into one another, unable to tell who was hurt and who did the hurting. But worse, unable to pick Rio out from the crowd, though I knew he was in the thick of it.

And then a huge hulking form snarled and sent a body flying backwards, and I knew that I had found him. "Rio!" I shouted. His head turned, then he was punching his way out of the crowd. He blocked a knife with his arm, its serrated blade leaving a jagged line of red along his forearm, before slamming his head into the forehead of his attacker. Then he was free, rushing back toward me. Blood trickled from a cut on his forehead and from the corner of his mouth.

"Come, there is no time." His voice was hard, and angry.

"I have to get to the exit, the guards will-"

He silenced me with a shake of his mane. "Not now. Not during this. They won't set foot in the prison when there's a riot, and if they didn't open the gate for their own men, they certainly won't do it for you. They'll bring down the riot doors and wait until everything has settled, until the damage is done and the crowd has burned itself out. What you *need* to do is go upstairs. We will be safe there."

His arm wrapped around my waist, and then he was dragging me through the people. I wanted to deny the truth and to insist that they would let me out, but I had the sinking feeling that he was right.

Most of the people were moving against us and toward the center of the conflict. It was like a dam of dissent had broken, and everyone rushed in to fill the void. Only the very young fled away from the mess. The children, Rio and myself.

When we reached Rio's tiny fortress, he slammed the door and locked it behind us. Shortly after, there was a knock, and after a few short, terse words another person entered the room—the small, dark skinned cook who had fed me the night before. Rio introduced him as Lumen, his second in command.

"Ay, Rio, you need to hear this," he said, his voice was tight with concern. He was clutching at an old battery operated radio which he waved frantically. Rio grabbed for it and the two huddled together, listening to short, staccato bursts of chatter which made no sense to me.

"What's happening?" I demanded.

"We can pick up the guard radio frequency, sometimes," Lumen answered. "And there's an awful lot of chatter."

"About the riot?"

Lumen hesitated, then shook his head.

"Then what?"

I wasn't sure I wanted the answer, particularly when Rio looked to me in alarm after one extended snatch of conversation, and Lumen sucked in a violent breath.

"The guard who let you into the prison. Was it the same guard who called out to me on the gate? The one with the tattoo of the tear beneath his eye?"

I shook my head. "It was someone else."

"Who?" Rio asked, leaning forward.

"Umm, I never got his name, but…" I thought hard. "That other guard, from last night. He said his name was Enrique, I think."

Rio and Lumen looked at each other.

"What," I said. "What's going on?"

"Why don't you take a seat?" Rio said gently.

A chill ran through me. No one ever got told to *take a seat* unless the news was very, very bad. "What happened? Was one of them injured in the riots?"

Rio grimaced. "Enrique was. He's in a coma, but they think he'll live."

I felt terrible for the wash of relief that swept through me at Rio's words. He hadn't said *two* guards were in a coma. "That means the other guard is okay, right? He can let me out, when the riots are over?"

That look again, between Rio and his offsider. "He's not a nice man, Bella. I had a run in with him myself."

"I know that," I said impatiently. "He left me locked in prison overnight, remember?" I crossed my arms. "But that was just for one night, to get back at you. What's going on?"

"He upset a lot of people. A lot of inmates, some of who aren't as... nice... as myself."

A terrible stone of dread settled in the pit of my stomach. It was a hot day, but I was suddenly cold. "What?" I said thickly, forcing myself to talk. "You said only one guard was injured."

"I said only one was in a coma. But there were three trapped inside the prison when the riot gates came down. One of them has minor injuries." He grew grim. "The other, the one with the tear tattoo, was stabbed 37 times."

Now I did stagger backwards, my hands reaching behind me for the bed. I sat down heavily upon it. "But he's alive, right?" I asked, already knowing the answer. Because if only two people knew I didn't belong here, and one was in a coma and the other was dead....

Rio shook his head sadly. He let the import of what had just happened sink in for a moment, then crossed to sit beside me on the bed.

"Bella. We'll find a way."

"How?" I asked, my voice rising. "Are we going to climb over the walls? Maybe dig a tunnel? *Hide in a bag of laundry?*"

Lumen tentatively raised his hand. "We could play the white card? Try and get her special treatment."

Rio shook his head. "There are a few white supremacists in prison, not many, but enough. They stick to themselves. The only thing unusual about Bella is that she's associating with 'the natives' and not banding together with them." He looked at me, brow furrowing. "Maybe that's something we should think about-

"Not a chance," I said, sickened at the thought. I'd had enough bigotry in one dinner with Gateau to last a lifetime. I couldn't imagine seeking protection with people like that.

He nodded, letting out a breath. "I had to ask—for your sake." His finger traced his scar. "I have some contacts, among the good guards. They might be able to help."

Because prison guards always believed the people inside when they said they weren't criminals, didn't they? But I didn't say that. Instead, I just nodded, numbly staring at the wall.

At my silence, Rio and Lumen glanced at each other, worry etched on both their faces.

"I'll go and see what I can find out," Rio said softly.

I continued to stare at the wall.

"Would you like Lumen to stay here and keep you company?"

I wrapped my arms around myself, and shook my head. "I think I'd like to be alone, please."

They exchanged a look again, and then Rio nodded. "We won't be long."

I sat in silence after they had left, then dropped back on the bed and closed my eyes. There wasn't anything I could do about being here, but maybe I could buy myself some time by pretending it wasn't happening.

I wasn't above doing that if it would grant me a few moments of peace.

***

When I woke, the sun was past its high point for the day. It seemed impossible that I could have slept so many hours away. I guess I had hoped I would wake up and things might be different—but they weren't.

Rio was sitting quietly against a wall, waiting for me to awake.

"Was it just a dream?" I croaked.

He shook his head. "The riot happened."

Tears burned behind my eyes, but I wouldn't let them come. "What did you find out?"

"The riots are burnt out, but the guards haven't yet returned. When order restores, we will bribe one of them to get a message out. Do you have anyone that you can contact?"

I nodded. "My father. He's the ambassador, here."

"That's good!" Rio said, as if to a child. "If we can get a message to him, he'll have some clout. You won't be here forever. Not like… well. You'll be back where you belong, soon enough."

Not like him. That's what he'd been about to say. I sniffed, wiping at my eyes, and sat up straight in bed. Here I was, worried about spending a couple of days in prison. And he'd spent how many? The haunted look in his eyes—it said they were too many to count.

"It was me, wasn't it?" I said. Deep down, I just knew. The riot had started, somehow, because of me.

Rio shook his head. "Of course not." But he wouldn't look me in the eye.

I sighed. "If I'm stuck here, I might as well know what I've done. Tell me."

He strode to the balcony doors, looking outside. The sun was hot, and the sky a flawless blue. From up here, away from the noise below, you'd think there had never been a riot at all. "It was my fault, not yours."

"How? You were with me when the riot started."

He drew a deep breath, as if trying to work out where to start, then turned to face me. "The prison works on a delicate balance, I think I told you that."

I nodded.

"And the courtyard is the largest area in the prison. All the gangs own a piece." Rio hesitated, choosing his next words carefully. "When I fought the Razors, yesterday, I was on their turf-"

A horrible realization came to me. My breath sucked in with a gasp as I realized where the conversation was going. "The other gangs saw them as weak, didn't they?" I said, my eyes widening. "You upset the balance."

Rio nodded. "By taking something from the Razors on their own ground, I invited other people to do it too. I created a turf war."

My eyes closed. It was hard to summon the strength to finish the chain of logic which came next. "You wouldn't have been there if it wasn't for me," I said. So much death. So much killing. It was all my fault.

He moved close. "You didn't know."

Hair fell over my eyes as I shook my head, pulling my knees up so that I could wrap my arms around them. "That's no excuse. I was a spoiled little rich girl, looking for adventure. I should never have bribed my way inside."

Rio passed a sidelong glance at me. "It's not all bad. There was last night."

He was sweet, this stranger who I suddenly knew so well. I moved over a little more, tapping the space beside me on the bed.

His mouth quirked up into a smile. "Oh. Are you inviting me into my own bed now?"

The smile that touched my lips was unintentional—he was trying to cheer me up, and despite my best efforts to remain miserable, it was working. I gave a little shrug. "Perhaps."

Rio settled back onto the bed next to me, stretching out and crossing his legs at the ankle, as though the disappointments and setbacks in the day barely meant anything to him.

I twisted toward him, unclasping my hands from around my legs so that I could run my fingers over his face. Up close I could trace the line of his scar, somehow fierce and representative of his vulnerability at the same time.

One eyebrow lifted, just like the corner of his mouth. "Ah, I see you are in the mood for a repeat performance."

My hand pushed him away. "I most certainly am not," I lied. "I just appreciate the company."

"You've got it, then."

In the light I studied him up close for the first time. His arms were exposed, and I could see the dark lines of ink peeking out from beneath the cotton of his shirt.

I slipped one hand under the sleeve, pulling it up for a better view. "You have so many," I said, studying the angry face of a dragon on his arm, its tail spiraling over the curve of his bicep.

He watched as my fingers traced the animal. "I do. I have one for every time I've been challenged. The loser chooses the animal."

"A dragon?"

This time he broke into a wolfish smile, his eyes gleaming. I could see why they called him el Lobo.

"No. This one picked a rat. He thought it would be punishment to have one on my skin forever. He did not realize however that a pair of wings could transform it into something else. I become the dragon, and he, the rat. I keep track of them that way. The men. The gangs. Living art that tells my history."

"Can I see the others?" I asked, though I knew we were entering dangerous territory. Getting to know Rio like this would only make it harder to walk away from him when I eventually left prison. And it wasn't going to help me forget last night, or what had happened this morning. It certainly wasn't going to keep me from wanting to do it again.

Rio gave another careless shrug and pulled himself forward enough to tug his shirt over his head, leaving his torso exposed.

They were everywhere. Like a tapestry of his life, little snapshots of one animal overcoming another. Once he was a bear, a wolf, a lion with a full mane. The tattoos were intricate and beautiful, and I couldn't imagine where he found an artist or supplies for something like that here inside the walls of the prison.

On his right shoulder, in a rare patch of space, a clock face sat, it's surface shattered and broken. I stared at it, head tilted, until I realized the numbers counted backwards. "If you could turn back time?" I asked, running my fingers counter-clockwise across it.

He nodded. "You already know me so well."

My fingers traced along his collarbone, and then down his broad chest. They paused at a scarred area covered in a tattoo that I'd initially mistaken for a quote in a foreign language. Fresh from gazing at the clock, I now realized the script was the word *Love* inscribed backwards.

"What happened here?"

Rio's hands moved over mine, stilling my fingers as they traced the ragged outline. His voice became hard. "I had a tattoo removed."

My brow furrowed. "Why? How?"

"The only way you can in prison," he snapped. "I scraped it off, then put something more appropriate over the top."

A shudder slipped through me as I was suddenly reminded of where we were. A prison where inmates could be stabbed with impunity, and the guards just locked the doors.

"But, why?" I pushed. I couldn't think of a single reason he would mutilate himself to remove a tattoo then just go and get a new one. No doubt the previous one had been as beautiful as the others. "What was the tattoo of?"

He pulled my hand from his chest, setting it down with a thump between us on the mattress. "Enough!"

Silence stretched between us, the moment destroyed, and I turned my back away from him. Maybe it was foolish, to leave myself vulnerable like that, but I couldn't bear him to see my face—to let him know how his brusqueness had stung.

My hands tucked beneath my cheek. The quiet of the room was now oppressively loud. For just a minute, I thought I felt my hair slide through a set of fingers, but I dismissed the notion as fantasy.

11: RIO

Two nights ago, she'd been the kind of gift you only dreamt about in prison. She'd been just as eager to please, as to be pleased.

Yesterday morning, of course, had not gone as well as I might have hoped. That couldn't be helped—it had been out of my hands, and only my hands had saved it from getting worse. But the afternoon? That had been my fault. Like a fool, I'd snapped at a simple, harmless question. She wasn't to know how much the answer had hurt. It seemed Elizabeth, the name etched beneath the scar, still haunted me. I could hear her laughter even now, and see those smoking guns. But that wasn't Bella's fault. How did I ever explain that the scar on my body was a mere shadow of the damage in my heart?

She'd kept her back to me the whole night, the line of her spine hard and rigid. Now, with another day fresh before us, I vowed to get her out of prison as soon as I could—for my sake, as well as hers. I thought back to Elizabeth, and that scar. A woman was the very reason I was in el Castillo. I would not let another woman destroy my life again.

I slipped from the bed before dawn, returning several hours later as Bella awoke.

Her cheeks were flushed and her hair tumbled over her shoulders in cascading waves. The memory of pushing that hair back to kiss her skin right where that pink met the slope of her jaw came back, unbidden. It brought a rush of desire with it that I knew I couldn't pursue.

She reached to adjust her skirt, her clothing askew, one creamy thigh exposed. That sight brought back memories as well.

"Come," I said briskly, more irritated with myself than with her. "It is time for breakfast."

"Where were you?"

"That's not important."

She looked at me doubtfully. "Won't that upset the Razors—me going outside again?"

I shook my head curtly. "It is fixed." It seemed this time, she knew better than to ask more questions about it.

She flipped back the sheets and hauled herself out of their depths. I handed her a bottle water, and she drank deeply. In this place where life was cheap, clean water was expensive. The prison had been designed for perhaps a tenth of the population it now supported. The sewerage system and the drinking water both groaned under the weight of far too many people. Those who drank from the one public well, or the taps in the toilet, frequently got sick.

For those who could afford it, rain barrels lined the courtyard, bringing clean water from the sky. It was why the gangs fought over the public space so fiercely. I traded what I could for water, after the rains. The gangs also sold drugs and woman, but I refused to allow either of those in my areas—or at least I had until recently.

Bella splashed her face, once she had drunk her fill—I gritted my teeth at the wastefulness, but said nothing. *She wasn't to know.* Then she took the toothbrush I offered and watched me through narrowed eyes as she brushed her teeth. It was obvious she still pondered all the reasons she shouldn't be with me, shouldn't be thinking about me. *I couldn't blame her.*

I had been thinking those same things. But unlike her, separating that piece of knowledge from the lust in my heart and loins was easier said than done. It had been a long time since sex had been more than just a perfunctory act. A long time since a woman had fallen asleep in my arms. I still reeled from the experience.

When she finished readying, we stepped out into the stairwell. The prison got louder as we journeyed down, the riot of the night before replaced now with chatter and laughter and the calls of friends. People moved back and forth, children playing tag through the corridors. It took a while to get used to, but in the end, this place was less a prison, and more a self-contained town.

It was a town you could never leave, and had very little control over, but a town nonetheless.

"The people here seem happy," Bella said, looking around her, as we moved through a corridor.

I shrugged. "This is my ward," I gestured around us. "You will never have any problems here. These people are my friends. I protect them. The gangs stay away. There are no drugs."

"It's a problem here?"

I nodded. Drugs had seeped into the prison. I'd even done my part, under duress, to aid the process—there was no choice when the prison warden was the man at the top of the ring. But that didn't mean I wished to be a part of the system, or would allow them within my ward.

I was one of the few left that resisted—drugs brought money to those at the top. But I'd seen firsthand what cocaine did to a person, and I didn't want that for those under my protection. "It would be easier to give in, but sometimes, you have to stand up for what is right." The people I looked after still had hope. Looking after them gave me hope in return, on days when it seemed like there was no hope at all.

My eyes narrowed as we rounded a corner, and I saw a man pressing a woman into a dark corner. I growled.

"What?" asked Bella.

"Nothing."

But she followed my gaze, focusing on the man and the woman. The man was a stranger. He had a freshly shaved head, and tattoos running up one arm.

But the woman, I recognized. She wore red lipstick and cheap makeup, with hair that went up, and cleavage that went down. A long slit had been cut in the thigh of her threadbare dress. One of the skinhead's hands were currently inside it.

I growled again.

"Are you going to do anything?" Bella asked, looking to me.

I shook my head. "After what happened when you arrived, I can't."

Her mouth turned down. When she looked at me, there was disdain in her eyes. "So, you'll just let her get raped?"

"It's not like that, Bella."

"Like hell it isn't," she said, hitching up her skirt. I reached out, but missed her by inches as she strode forward, an exploding firework.

"Hey you!" she called in a commanding tone. The man and woman looked up at her approach. Shock registered on both their faces.

"Get away from that woman. *Now.*" Bella's voice bit like the edge of a blade. Even I missed a step at the power behind her tone.

The skinhead didn't take the hint. He stepped away from the girl and bobbed his head toward Bella, examining this new curiosity. His smile curled into something cruel and hungry, a hand reaching inside his jacket pocket.

She stepped toward him and his smile vanished. He stepped back, looking above her head. And then ran for his life.

Bella turned to me in triumph, crowing her victory, but stopped short when she discovered me standing directly behind her, arms crossed. Her posture slumped as she realized what the man had really backed away from—a big, nasty, tattoo covered dog. Not her, the overeager pup.

The girl looked at Bella for a moment with sad eyes.

Bella, naturally, misread them. "Are you alright? Did he hurt you?"

"You must be new," the girl said, smiling in that way people reserve for those that mean well.

"How did you guess?"

She slid the back of her fingers across Bella's cheek. "Bless you."

Then her eyes flicked to me. "El Lobo," she said softly. "How's Mateo?"

"He misses his mother," I said, arms folded.

Her smile faltered, but only for a moment. Then she turned and walked away, reestablishing her dignity in the sway of her hips.

Bella's face creased. "What was that about?"

"She wasn't being raped, Bella."

"What do you mean?"

I remained silent, letting her work it out.

Realization slowly dawned on her face in equal parts embarrassment and horror. "She was a prostitute?"

I nodded.

The red in her cheek burned hotter. "You let them work here?"

I sighed, uncrossing my arms at last to run one hand through my hair. "I do now."

"Since when?"

"This morning."

Her mouth dropped open for the second time in as many minutes. "The reason you were out?"

I nodded.

"The reason you said I was safe?"

I nodded again. "I made a deal with the Razors. They stay away from you, I let their women work my area."

A hundred questions flashed across her eyes. It took her several moments to sort through and work out which she wanted to ask. "Who are these Razors, Rio?"

A shiver ran down my spine. Few people used my real name so casually. Even the guards called me *the Wolf*. "They rule the prison," I said, stamping down the emotions that bubbled at the sound of my name on her lips. "Or, parts of it. There are kingdoms within el Castillo. The Razors control the central area, and parts of the Apex—a slum area of the prison set against the east wall. They built their power on controlling the prostitution trade. They have more men than all the other gangs combined."

I motioned for her to continue walking. We moved side by side down the corridor, her little legs almost running to keep up with my long strides.

"There are other gangs?"

I nodded. "The guards control the drug trade. *Nuestra Familia* control the largest water supply. Mafia control most of the West side.

"And you?" Bella asked softly. "What do you control?"

My footsteps faltered. "My rage," I said at last.

She cocked her head, trying to understand.

"When I get angry… I see red," I muttered. "The rage scares people—it's uncontrollable. When I go berserk…" I drew a deep breath, trying to explain. "Well, it's like the guards, right? There are 20 times as many men in Diego's gang as there are law enforcement. The guards need to rule by fear. If they didn't, they wouldn't have a chance. When a guard enters a prison carrying riot gear and guns, everyone backs away, because of *fear*. Even though the prisoners have the advantage of numbers, no one wants to be the martyr who gets killed first."

I bared my teeth. "The other gangs look at me like that. No one wants to be the first, or second, or third person to die. My fury keeps me safe."

Her head tilted to one side as her brows drew together. "And so, you've carved out your own little empire."

"I do what I can to keep my people safe. I run… errands… for the guards. I own the gym. And now, I allow the Razors to pedal their wares. I guess that's a good thing, in the end."

"How so?"

"I've been thinking about it for a while now. The Razors, they use drugs to fish for women," I said. "A little bit of coke on the side, and the next thing you know, girls like Ezzi back there are so imbedded in it that they can't live without it. Once that happens, the Razors own you. They have their prostitutes. And they use them to bring in more users, more worker bees."

I shrugged as we moved down the hall, past curtained domiciles to the left and right. It was bleak, but that was the way life was—no point in denying the facts. Bella would learn that quickly here in el Castillo. "At least in my area I can ensure they will be treated well. I've made it known that anyone mistreating a prostitute answers directly to me."

We walked in silence until I saw my second in command weaving toward us. I nodded toward the boy. "There's Lumen. Perhaps he has news about the guards."

I called to him but he didn't stop. He moved quickly, with his head down, and his eyes when they flashed up at me were urgent. "Best be scarce," he muttered as he flew past.

I snagged Bella's elbow and pressed her into the open door of an empty cell just in time to see a group of guards in full riot gear burst from a doorway just ahead. A struggling man was held between them as a third, sporting a fully automatic rifle, hung a set of rosary beads from a hook upon the wall.

"*A Dios mio,*" I said before I could stop myself. I made the sign of the cross.

Bella's voice was urgent and worried. "What?" she asked, her face half hidden in the shadows.

I shuddered. There were few things in prison I was truly afraid of. *This was one of them.* "The *rosario.* The mark of the damned."

"What do you mean?" she whispered.

I looked to the rosary beads, still swaying gently, clinking against the concrete of the wall further up the corridor ahead. "They hang the beads on the door when a prisoner is to be executed. It marks his final seven days. He is being taken to another cell. He has one week to live."

She gasped, her face blanching. I realized I still held her by the arm, but when I let her go, she clutched at me in return.

"That's horrible."

I nodded. "It's the only time the guards venture into the prison—for executions. They hang beads on a door, then reappear 7 days later to finish the job."

"What did that man do?" she finally murmured.

It was a good question, and one I had also been pondering. "Repercussions for yesterday, perhaps."

But even while saying it, I frowned. The guards had been armed to the teeth, which supported my claim. But I knew the man vaguely. He wasn't a member of the major gangs—he kept to himself; didn't drink, didn't do drugs.

I pulled Bella out into the hallway as soon as the guards had disappeared. Lumen had made it further down the hall and was still pressed up against the wall when we arrived.

I jerked my head in his direction and he fell in step beside me. When we were back in my room I pushed the door closed behind us, the three of us submerged in the most privacy we could ever hope to have in the prison.

"What is going on?" I hissed. "Why was that man taken? What was his crime?" It was ironic to say these words in prison, like we had all been blameless to begin with. But I wasn't talking about why the man had been brought here now, rather the reason he was about to be taken out.

Lumen shrugged. "Man, I don't know. They're saying it's because of yesterday. That he was a ringleader."

"Bullshit."

"I know." He looked at me, his eyes flicking to Bella nervously, then swallowed.

"What is it?"

"Rio, I'm hearing stories."

"What kind of stories?"

"That the Warden's drug sales are drying up."

I frowned. Lumen's words confirmed the price hikes in the cafeteria stalls. But what did it have to do with this? "And?"

"And what if he's found another way to make money, Rio?"

"Like what?"

"Well it's only chatter I heard on the radio, but…" he drifted off.

I raised one eyebrow. "Spit it out."

"The guards have strict instructions not to beat the prisoner," Lumen blurted. "Especially around the kidneys. The Warden gave the message personally."

My frown deepened. That was unusual. Usually the guards could care less about trying to hurt us. Specific commands to avoid violence were rare. And why, of all things, the kidneys?

What if he's found another way to make money, Rio? Lumen's words drifted back to me as the entire perspective of my world began to turn. There was only one reason you didn't want damage to a dying man's organs. I looked to Bella and swallowed. *A Dios mio.* What had I gotten this woman into?

12: BELLA

I kicked myself for *ever* imagining that there would be something romantic or fairytale-like about the inside of a prison. There wasn't. Not even close. I walked laps around Rio's room, slamming my palm on the door each time I passed in frustration. Each minute that ticked by seemed to bring with it more thoughts I wanted to banish from my mind—more I couldn't escape.

Rio had refused to tell me his theory about why the prisoner was taken, but I'd pieced it together with a few key questions to Lumen. When he'd told me, his speech low, as if ashamed to even voice his theory, my face had gone so pale I could have been dead myself. How could a system be so corrupt that the people within it would nod their heads and believe, even just for a moment, that harvesting healthy organs from prisoners by sentencing them to death was acceptable at any level?

It was something out of a bad horror movie, or one of those trashy tabloids my father's cleaners read from the bottom rung of the magazine shelf. I couldn't wrap my mind around it.

Rio and Lumen had huddled, speaking quickly in Spanish. When they parted, determination creased their brows. It was more urgent than ever to get a message about me out. I'd nodded in terrified agreement as they said they would leave me here and see what they could do.

Now, as I waited for their return, I walked in a tight circle around the room, hitting the door jamb each time I passed as implications bloomed in my thoughts. Might Gateau know the truth? He had said he knew the inner workings of the prison, and certainly his name had worked on the door. If that were true, was he somehow involved?

I refused to accept it. Gateau hadn't struck me as the most conscientious man in the world, but... but... The way he'd talked about the prisoners here, over dinner, as if they were animals. My mind whirled. I was trapped here, and the more I heard, the more I wanted to get out. I'd go to Gateau, demand the truth. And then see my father—surely, he had some pull as well. I slammed the door again as I passed. I'd been such a fool to leave no indication at all about where I would be.

As though it would have killed me to leave a note for my father on my dresser.

Rio had forbidden me to leave the room without an escort—not that I planned on doing that. There had once been payphones, Rio told me, but they had long since been ripped from the wall for the quarters they contained. A few of the prisoners had cell phones, but when my eyes lit up, he shook his head—using one indebted you to the owner, and they would demand things of my body that Rio did not want me to pay. Our best bet was the guards. With them now in the prison again, for whatever nefarious purpose that might be, he would see if one could be bribed.

A scrabble at the door set my heart racing, before it opened and Rio's familiar figure appeared.

"I have news."

"Yes?" I asked quickly, rushing to him.

"I found a guard."

A knot I hadn't realized had been twisting my insides tightened. "And?"

Rio smiled. "It cost me, but he can be bribed."

"He can get me out?"

He shook his head. "He'll get a message out. I'm sorry. It's as much as he will do."

"Thank you," I said. My knees were shaking. I lowered myself carefully to sit on the bed.

"What did you give him?" I asked.

He shook his head again, walking to the double doors, opening them to look out into afternoon sun. "It doesn't matter."

"Did you give him money?" I asked, standing, to walk to him.

He shook his head a third time. "There is precious little of that, in here. I gave him something more important."

"What's that?"

He turned to face me, the look of pain that flashed behind his eyes quickly hidden. "I gave him power."

I looked at Rio, trying to decipher the meaning behind his words. Rio controlled almost a quarter of the prison population. Whatever it had been, the price had been steep. *And he'd paid it for me.*

"You're not… you're not going to kill anyone, are you?"

He shook his shaggy mane of hair. I'd ceased being amazed when I said something that was preposterous, but was so common here people considered it seriously. "No. And he can't run drugs through my area either, I drew the line at that." He walked out onto the balcony, his fingers gripping the railing until they turned white. "But from now until hell freezes over, I'll be his lapdog. I'll come at his bidding, escort him through my areas, give him access to my people. I'll organize prostitutes for all the guards, daily. I'll lick his boots if he asks me to."

I followed him outside. Rio was a proud man. To do such a thing... "I'm sorry," I whispered, standing at the railing beside him.

He shook his head. "I'm not. I'd have done far worse, if he'd asked." His eyes were deep, and soulful. Those same eyes I'd seen in the market, the first time we'd met. "I'd do anything, for you."

My hands drifted over his, at the railing. "How can I ever repay you?"

Now he smiled, one hand catching mine. "You already have. That first night... I'll remember it always."

He turned toward me, and I moved into him, an idea forming. "Will the guard get an answer back to you, tonight?"

He shook his head.

"Then," I said, leaning up to kiss him ever so softly on the lips before sliding onto my knees before him, "let's make some more memories, just to pass the time."

He growled, and I saw one hand tighten on the balcony, his fingers white, like before, when he realized my intentions.

I bit my lip as I worked at his belt. This man had been so good to me. No, better than that. He'd been a hero in the most unexpected of places. He'd saved my life countless times now, and was in the process of doing it once again. That first night, before we made love, he'd come to this balcony, staring out at a city he could never meet. Perhaps, in my own small way, I could give him the gift of happier thoughts, the next time he stood in this spot.

I worked his pants down his hips, the afternoon sunshine hot on my back, discovering a heat between my own legs at the thought of what I was about to do. We were out in the open, but alone—higher than most; far above the prison below. My fingers traced a crease in his shorts. It would be a public act, but also private.

Beneath the cotton, he'd already begun to swell. I caressed his bulge - eliciting a low growl from above — before pulling his shorts down and freeing the beast.

My God. I'd felt it that first night, in my hand and in my body. I'd known he was big—proportional to every other muscle in his massive body. But to see it up close! I took him tenderly in one hand, enjoying the view as I watched him swell. *I'd taken this inside me?*

Its color was slightly lighter than the rest of his tanned body; both soft and hard at the same time—full of give when I squeezed, though rapidly gaining resistance. Already it didn't fit comfortably in my palm, lengthening as it swelled, a small bead of moisture on the tip.

I leaned close, licking it off. It was salty; like sweat but different—stronger, reminiscent of the sex it precipitated. Heat bloomed between my thighs, and I reached down, placing a hand between them at the thought.

My tongue lapped out again. His member jerked at its touch, the last vestiges of softness flying away as he gasped. As one hand slowly stroked myself, my lips lowered upon him. Hot breath, then moist lips. My tongue wrapped around his head as my jaw widened.

He was big. But if I'd taken him before, between my legs, I could take at least some of him now within my mouth. I slid down, just a little, then back up, moistening him. My free hand took him at his base then rose to meet me as I descended once again.

Above me, Rio groaned. He tried to pull me up. I shook my head. "This is all about you," I murmured, slipping off him to look up. "A memory I don't want you to forget."

His hands tightened on my shoulders as I slid back down, lips and hand working in unison. *It wasn't all about him, though.* At my hips, my legs widened. My skirt was bunched at my waist; the fingers of my other hand beneath my panties. I stroked myself in time to my strokes above. When he began to breathe faster, I quickened both.

A spike of pleasure shot through me, and my shoulders hunched. This shouldn't feel so good! I should be pleasuring him! But I didn't stop my fingers. Instead, I moved quicker again. Though I didn't have him between my legs, I had him inside my mouth. I could taste him, and lick him, and suck him, and the knowledge that it was my lips that were making him grip the railing beside me was a thrill unto itself.

The heat between my legs spread through my body. I could feel my heart in my throat, and it came out in moans around him, shooting vibrations down his shaft. Oh God. It was becoming so hard to concentrate. All I wanted to do was let him go and lie back and spread my legs.

But I kept going. This was for him as well as for me. Eyes wide in pleasure, my fingers gripping his shaft, I continued to work my mouth harder than my fingers below.

The first blissful stabs of impending orgasm shot through me. I doubled over, my hand clenching tighter upon him, another moan issuing from my mouth. Rio groaned. When I looked up, his head was raised to the heavens. "I can't take much more of this Bella," he warned.

Good. I wanted to tell him. *You and me both.*

Another spike shot through me—lightning striking the same ground twice. I doubled over, eyes rolling, fighting to keep my hand tight as it flashed upon him.

"Bella…" His huge form tensed above me. I tasted the first hot warning in my mouth.

Oh God. I wanted this so much. I sucked with all my might, gazing up that magnificent, muscled body as below, my fingers dove inside. And suddenly, he was looking down, his eyes wide, and he was swelling within my mouth.

A hot rush hit my tongue as we both cried out—his voice a roar into the sky, mine muffled pleasure as I drank both our orgasms in. His hard, jerking member drove my own pleasure higher, defining it, multiplying it. I shook on the ground, eventually having to pull away as my body hunched and my entire focus became the flames between my legs. When I looked up, blinking back tears, he was leaning back against the balcony, eyes wide with shock.

The tiniest, finest cobweb of saliva still linked us. I followed it back to his member, my tongue flicking against the velvety flesh and tasting him once more. I looked up and bit my lip. "Did you like that?"

He pulled me up into a fierce embrace. "I'll never look out from this balcony and think of anything but that, ever again."

13: RIO

I padded out of the room as the sun rose—Bella's naked, nubile form curled up between the sheets. It had taken long, delicious minutes to untangle her from around my neck and body, and I'd faltered more than once as I lifted a draped arm. How easy it would be to go back to bed—to ignore the world's troubles in the soft skin and jasmine scent beside me.

But there were people who relied upon me. I couldn't afford that luxury. And so, I strode down the stairs and along corridors until I could be where my people needed me the most.

The gym.

The other leaders had yet to arrive. Nuestra Familia, the South American Mafia, the Razors. I'd even invited the White Supremacists, though I detested them more than most. Everybody had said they would answer my call.

I worked out while I waited for them to arrive, picking up a length of rope to skip briefly for cardio before moving onto weights—dumbbells made from concrete and iron that

I curled and pushed above my chest. I was almost at the limits of what the gym could provide. Soon I would have to work out a way to add extra weight.

Bella. My attraction to her had been instant, right from the start. From that first time I'd set eyes on her in the market, I'd feared for where she might take me. I was a creature of anger. Feared. That was how I survived. But Bella? She looked at me differently to everyone else. In a way that made me want to stop being angry.

Last night had been… magical. First the balcony, and then her body, wrapped around mine, for hours after. It was as if the storm of our previous disagreements had passed, leaving only sweet air in its wake.

I drew another breath, exerting myself as I heaved concrete and iron above my chest. I'd do anything for her. My body was already strong, but I'd make it stronger. I'd build treaties. I'd negotiate with enemies. I'd make this prison safe, if she must remain within it.

"Your bicep must weigh more than me."

I looked up, sweat slicking my body, to see a familiar figure at the doorway. *I'd even welcome enemies with a smile.* "Come in."

Marika, the leader of Nuestra Familia, smiled at my words and approached. She was a thin woman with large breasts and soft lips, which pursed suggestively as she eyed my body.

I grunted, letting the weights I had been benching roll to the side. Her body might be soft, but she was a hard woman. Rumor had it she'd paid for her fake tits with insurance from her dead husband, shortly before being caught for his murder.

"There's no one else here," Marika said. "Did you invite me to have your way with me?"

"In your dreams," I growled. I stood, striding to pick up a towel recently liberated from Mateo's secret hideout. "The others will be here soon enough."

"Suit yourself," she murmured. Her eyes never left my body as I wiped down the hard muscle, my veins popping after my workout. She licked her lips. "I'm here if you change your mind."

The entry of another leader saved me a retort. Marika moved to one side, watching the newcomer warily. Raul, of the South American Mafioso.

None of us met often. My meeting had been called only because of extraordinary circumstances.

The other leaders soon joined us, Diego of the Razors arriving last of all. His was the largest gang and perhaps the most powerful, though I controlled the food and others controlled the water. He scowled when he saw me, fingering a bruise that still covered one eye.

"What are we doing here, el *Loco*."

I gritted my teeth at the barb, trying not to let my anger show. I hadn't been like this once—so quick to jump at a sharp comment. I'd laughed freely, and let things roll off my back.

You couldn't do that in prison, though. Power and image were everything. Let someone take a piece of that and you suffered the consequences.

I ignored Diego only with effort. "I'm here to suggest a truce."

Diego laughed. Even Marika snorted. But I shook my head. "The riots of three days ago can't happen again. The Warden is up to something. We need to start working together to stand strong."

Diego spat to one side. "We're already strong. But if you're suggesting you aren't..." he bared his teeth.

My anger rose again at his challenge. This time it was harder to push back down. I did it only by thinking of Bella, and how she needed to be protected. Of her soft skin, and what she'd done for me, last night. "Even you, Diego. We need even you. The Warden is up to something. My people are going missing..."

Diego laughed. "Good!"

I snarled, my fists clenched, my face turning red. "Do not test me!" I said, spittle flying from my mouth. holding myself back only with straining effort. "You are my guest here, but that could soon change." A dull throbbing burned behind my eyes.

"Easy, big boy," Marika said. "We're here, aren't we? What are you suggesting."

I drew a deep breath. When I could speak again, I was calmer. "The courtyard. I want to make it neutral ground."

Several of the leaders burst out laughing. "Why would we do that?" said one.

"What do we get out of the deal?" asked another.

My fist clenched then unclenched. I forced it to relax, before the Red could envelope me.

"Something is going on, in el Castillo. You've all heard the stories. How many of you have had good people go missing in the last week?"

They looked from one to the other, suddenly sober.

"Two hundred and thirty-seven," I said softly. "That's how many people I care for."

"Well the riots-" began Raul.

"Eight of my people got injured in your riots!" I said, the Red flaring at my edges once again. He'd been one of the instigators. "Several of them almost died!"

I stalked toward him. "You lost seven." Then I rounded on Marika. "Nuestra Familia lost eight, and has another 20 injured." I looked to the leader of the white supremacists, an idiot with sunken eyes and a blue swastika tattooed upon his forehead. I stabbed him in the chest with my finger. "Even you lost someone in that fight," I said. I threw up my hands in frustration. "And all because some idiot wanted to take a little turf!"

I breathed deep, collecting myself. "I had people injured, but that's not the point. That's not why we're here." I grimaced. "Because eight got injured, but I'm missing 18 more." I looked at each of them in turn. "They didn't die in the riots. Do we really want to play these petty games and make it easier for the Warden to collect our bodies?"

Silence, from the group. Then Diego spat. "There's no proof he's harvesting organs. You know that."

I opened my mouth but it was Marika who spoke. "Four of my men, and one woman, got delivered Rosarios last night. All for crimes that have no merit."

Raul nodded. "I... have similar stories. Though I hear it's not the Warden doing the collecting, but someone else. Regardless, my people are going missing. Healthy people — never the sick."

I looked from one to the other. "Well? We may not like each other, but we have a duty to our people."

Diego scowled, but the rest looked ready to listen. "What do you suggest?" asked Marika.

"The courtyard becomes common property. All water barrel rights are retained by the original owners — people that mess with that suffer the consequences. But it's free for all to access — no more dividing it along invisible lines," I said. "And no more fighting, on pain of losing your territory."

Raul sucked in a breath. "That's some serious consequences."

"So is losing 18 of my best," I growled. "That riot got us nowhere. It only served to make us weaker, and the Warden stronger. Those guards that were injured are the perfect excuse to sentence as many as he wants to death." I looked from one to the other. "Well?"

Marika was the first to nod. "Deal."

Surprisingly, Diego, of the Razors, was second. "Agreed," he said. There was a look of calculation in his eyes.

As one by one, each of the other section leaders nodded in turn, the knot that had remained in my chest since the riot began to loosen. If we could work together, there might be hope for us yet.

14: BELLA

Morning brought with it a fresh dose of reality. I was in prison, and despite my best efforts, we couldn't spend the entire day making love.

When Rio returned from his workout, smelling of iron and sweat and all things deliciously manly, he washed at the water barrel, and then we moved to the balcony. Far below, people moved back and forth, going about their day chatting and running errands. Rio told me he'd met with the other gang leaders—I had no idea when that had happened—and negotiated communal rights to the courtyard. He let out a burst of laughter when I pointed out a few enterprising individuals who had already set up shop in one far corner.

Then his face fell. "So, think you'll be back to visit after you make it out of here?" he asked, flashing me a tight, strained grin. "Or will you never look back and forget all of us here at el Castillo?"

A brief surge of anger spiraled through me, and I opened my mouth to deny his words. But... what other choice was there? I wouldn't be able to stop by for a quick visit or a cup of tea, would I? "Rio, I..."

"It's okay," he said. "You're not meant for this life."

I took his hand. "Neither are you. You play the beast, but you can't fool me. You aren't meant for this either."

He looked down, over our balcony, a king above his subjects. "None of these people are," he said quietly. "Nobody deserves to live like this."

I followed his gaze, reassessing my earlier assumptions of the people below. They weren't spending a sunny afternoon milling through shops and running errands— they were barely getting by, clinging to life in a place that didn't want to see them live.

Surely, they didn't deserve that.

A group of children played a game on a patch of dirt that was slightly better maintained than the rest of the courtyard. I scanned the crowd for a parent nearby, someone responsible for looking over them.

"Are they always like that?" I asked, when I couldn't find anyone. "There's no one there to watch them."

He followed where I pointed to the group of kids.

Rio frowned. "No. There is usually a teacher. Sometimes more than one. Perhaps something has happened..." He shook his head as if dispelling a bad thought. "Who knows, Bella. There is so much right now that's uncertain. Perhaps they were injured in the riot. Or removed." The words were dark, and I knew we were both thinking of those rosary beads.

He growled in frustration. "I can fight for them. I can keep the predators at bay. But I can't fight the *Rosario*."

I gnawed on my lower lip, then looked up at him. "I want to go down to them. Will you take me?"

Rio wouldn't let me go down there alone. More than that, I didn't *want* to go down by myself. But... I couldn't imagine what it might feel like to be those children—to

93

have the person who usually helped them disappear without any explanation at all.

He studied me. I wasn't sure I really wanted to know what he was thinking, but I met his eyes anyway. Rio already had more access to me than anyone else had in a long time. To my body. To my insecurities. Could there really be anything wrong with a little bit of vulnerability?

His head tilted in a nod as he came to a decision. "You'll be safe if I'm around." A callused hand gestured to me. "Come."

Rio took me down to the courtyard, pausing in the shadows while I walked toward the children. "I'll be here," was all he said to my questioning glance.

"Hola!" I said nervously as I approached the children. Would they even want to say hello?

I glanced back for support from Rio. He was bending down, gesturing to a child with his hands. He waved at me, then pointed in my direction. The child ran toward the larger group of children, whose interest I'd already piqued.

"Hola! Hola!" a series of little voices chorused. They swarmed around me; like they had been waiting for the moment someone would take the time to greet them. It pulled at my heartstrings to see how little it took to garner such immediate affection from them. Prison or not, these were just children.

They began to introduce themselves, speaking over one another in their rush to tell me their names and to hear mine. Many of them were so young; I might be the first American they had ever seen.

I heard about their names and who their parents were, whether they had any siblings and how long they had been behind the prison walls.

"Why are you here?" I asked. I'd been wondering what possible crimes a child so young could have committed to be in prison.

"This is where we live," one said, pulling a face like I was the crazy one for asking.

I laughed, tousling her hair. "Yes, but what made you come. Why aren't you outside?"

The little one went quiet. "I've never been outside. What's it like?"

I frowned, puzzling through her answer. She'd never been outside? How could that be? Unless... "Your mama. She came here before you were born, didn't she?"

She nodded, and I sat back, rocking on my heels. "Oh, little one." This child. *All the grubby faces that surrounded me*—the only crime they'd committed was being born.

"Where's your mother?" I asked softly.

"Daddy's missing. Mama is looking for him."

After that, I stopped asking questions. But I couldn't walk away—not now. So we did the alphabet—I taught it to them in English, and they taught it back to me in Spanish—which I pretended not to know. They all laughed when I got the pronunciation wrong. We counted the stone blocks and windows that made up the outside of the prison. We looked up, and imagined the clouds in the sky were animals, and played games of tag and I Spy.

It wasn't until the sun had turned orange in the reflection of the guard tower that I realized how late it was. Rio had watched from the sidelines with a fond smile on his face, Lumen running messages to him so that he could conduct his business within eyesight. But as the children began to scatter, he came forward.

"Did you enjoy that?"

I nodded. Surprisingly, I had. Though the morning had started full of distress, I'd forgotten it as quickly as the children had with the myriad games we had played. Looking after those children, teaching them, had left me more satisfied than I'd felt in a long, long time.

One of the last children ran up to Rio as he approached. It was the same one who had run to him when I'd first arrived that morning. He tugged at Rio's sleeve. The other children had called him Mateo, and he had laughed and played along with the others, though he'd never said a word to me.

The giant dropped down so he was eye-level with the child. Mateo raised his hands and began to sign.

Rio glanced up at me and gave a crooked grin. "He says he had fun with you and thinks you're very pretty." An eyebrow quirked. "Don't worry. I won't be jealous."

Oh God. The child was deaf. *I was the worst teacher in the world.*

Mateo tapped at his ear, and I noticed a hearing aid. He shrugged, then glanced at Rio, signing a question. Rio shook his head sadly. Mateo gave a small nod and tipped his head as if to say, 'What can you do?'

A voice called out from behind us. "Mateo?"

Mateo slipped past me and into the arms of a woman I recognized. Heat rose in my cheeks. The woman from the corridor. *The prostitute.* I swallowed my embarrassment and walked over to Mateo and his mother before they could leave.

"Hello," I said. "Mateo had an excellent day."

"He's an excellent boy," she said. She looked past me at Rio, who nodded and looked away from us.

"It's Ezzi, right?"

"Yes," she said. "And you are Bella?"

"That's right."

She gave me that sad, *poor you* smile again. "People talk about you."

Mateo pulled at her arm and pointed at a group of children playing an impromptu game with a ball in the courtyard. "Yes, go ahead," Ezzi said, signing at him at the same time. Mateo joined the fray.

"I wanted to apologize," I said. "For interrupting your work the other day."

"It's no bother," she said. "That guy was a creep."

"I hope they're not all like that."

She shrugged, flashing me the same look Mateo had given Rio—*what can you do?*

We watched Mateo play with the children, the silence becoming more comfortable between us.

"Do you enjoy your job?" I asked, though I immediately felt stupid for asking.

She laughed. "It's a strange world," she said, as Mateo charged with the ball, scoring a point, though no one seemed to be counting. "I can't tell you I *enjoy* it. I don't like the creeps, and the guards are starting to get demanding. They bring in outsiders, too, sometimes. They're the worst, because they treat us like cattle—they know we can't complain."

Mateo caught her eye and flashed her a grin. She smiled back, her face suddenly alight. "But it's not all bad. It keeps my son fed, and as safe as he can be. And I've never been one for relationships." She looked at me sideways. "There are occasional fun times too—some people are better than others, you know how it is."

I looked to Rio. *Yes, I did know.*

She caught my look, and we shared a smile.

"You've got a good one there. He keeps so many of us safe."

I nodded, but then a horrifying thought occurred to me. "You and Rio. You haven't...?" I left the question hanging.

She laughed. "I wish. The offer is always on the table, but he's never taken it."

My body almost sagged with relief.

Rio returned when Ezzi and Mateo took their leave.

He stepped beside me. "What did you two chat about?"

I tried to make my shrug as nonchalant as possible. "This and that."

"Was today everything you thought it would be?"

I nodded. "It was. They're sweet kids."

"They are," Rio agreed.

"What was Mateo saying? I didn't realize… I just thought he was quiet."

He gave a careful shrug. "Mateo can hear with a hearing aide. But batteries are hard to come by here, and his last went flat a few weeks ago." He gave a frustrated growl, his eyes flashing with anger. I was suddenly back in that moment when I first laid eyes on him.

He'd given me a watch. My eyes went wide as I put two and two together. *Watches had batteries just the right size for a hearing aide.*

"Rio, I'm so sorry," I whispered.

He shook his head. "You weren't to know. That's why I didn't say anything."

I took his hand, and he smiled. We walked hand in hand toward the exit.

And, I realized, my own smile faltering, three Razor thugs.

15: RIO

The tug of her clenched hand in mine drew me to a halt.
The thugs lounged in the doorway like they owned it; three
goons with shaved heads and faces so pockmarked you'd
think they were moon craters. I recognized the leader,
Diego, by the black eye I'd given him the night he'd tried to
accost Bella.

"Get out of our way," I growled, tensing for a fight.

Diego shook his head. "Now, now, el Lobo, you should
know the agreement. You're the one who brokered it today.
The courtyard is common property—no fighting, on pain of
losing your territory."

He picked at a gap in his teeth with a long, dirty nail.
"So, that means we're allowed to be here. As long as we
don't stop you getting through, you can't stop us resting
against this wall."

I growled, but Bella's hand went to my shoulder, and I
remembered who I was with. "Let's get out of here," I said,
pushing past the thugs.

"That's right, walk away with your whore."

Fury ignited behind my eyes as I spun to face them, but Bella stepped between us again. "Rio, please," she said softly.

Though all I longed to do was crush the speaker's throat between my fingers, Bella's eyes drew me away. They were soft, and beautiful, and they drowned my anger in other emotions.

My fingers clenched, but then I spun and begun to stalk away.

"I see you like the children," Diego said conversationally to Bella as she passed. "Perhaps you would enjoy one of your own. I could help you with that, anytime."

With a roar, I strode quickly toward the *gilipollas*. The leer in Diego's eyes turned to triumph at my approach, but as my hands reached for his throat, Bella was there again.

"Rio. It's just words," she murmured. She reached out to touch my wrist. "Please. Let it go."

"That's right," Diego said, recovering his composure. His hands went to his crotch, and he gripped it. "Let it go…" His eyes narrowed, "like the pussy you are."

The Red enveloped me, consuming me, and I lunged toward the man without conscious thought, my entire mind filled with a vision of him purpling within my hands. A roar escaped my lips—a roar of fury, and the need to protect what was mine.

"I'll kill you!" My hands closed around his throat. His eyes went wide, and he scrabbled at me, but he couldn't find a purchase. I was dimly aware of his companions battering at either side, but I ignored them. In my rage, I was invulnerable. I couldn't be hurt, I couldn't be reasoned with, I couldn't be-

A soft hand fell across my bicep. A voice, so sweet that it made my heart ache, cut across the edges of the Red. "Rio. Don't do this."

I snarled. "He'll die for what he just said. And when he has, I'll tattoo him as a maggot upon my chest."

"No, you won't," the voice reasoned. There was a plea in it. And worry. And the thought that I might have caused that worry made my heart break. The Red dimmed further. "Please, listen to me. This is what they want. If you start a fight, now, they take your territory. By your own words!"

I snarled, but my heart wasn't in it. The Red was fading, reluctantly. Because the sweet voice was right.

Bella pulled me toward her as I released Diego. He fell back with a gasp, color returning to his face as his hands went to his throat.

She smiled softly. "You'd never let them win so easily. Who would protect me, or the children?"

Looking into her eyes, I slowly nodded. The tension left my shoulders. My fists began to unclench.

Diego and his goons scrambled back. "You fought! You broke the truce!"

My fists clenched, the Red returning, but it was Bella who rounded on them. "You think this was a fight?" she said, stalking toward them. They stepped back again. "This wasn't a fight. This was a *warning*."

She stabbed out a finger, jabbing the leader in the chest. "You picked the fight, not him. Do it again, and face *the Beast*." She spun on her heels, striding back toward me. "Come on Rio. These *idiotas* aren't worth our time."

I ached to fight, to smash heads and lose myself in anger. But Bella... she lay a gentle hand on my arm. "Rio, please," she whispered. "Anger doesn't have to be the only way." The look of pleading in her eyes... that look that said she believed in me—that I was more than just flesh and bone bound by anger—it held the Red back. I struggled not to give in. I struggled to be... human.

And as the Red retreated—not gone, but held now at bay—I saw what Bella, with her cool head—had seen from the start. These men were baiting me, relying on my anger to do what they couldn't do on their own—take my territory. I glared at them one last time, fists clenching to hold back my rage, before turning to stride beside Bella through the arches.

When I looked back, Diego and his gang were still scratching their heads, trying to work out what had gone wrong.

16: BELLA

Rio seethed. I'd stopped him, made him see sense, but the anger hadn't disappeared. His shoulders were still hard, his step an angry stalk. Until we were back in his room, he said nothing at all.

Once we were there, the door closed and the two of us safely sequestered, he paced back and forth, refusing to look at me.

I sat on the chair in the corner. It wouldn't do either one of us any good to interrupt him. I would have to wait until he was ready to come down on his own.

When he finally stopped his pacing, he dropped down onto the bed, not looking in my direction.

I gave him another minute. Two. And then I crossed the space separating us and joined him.

Another beat passed, sitting next to one another; not touching, barely coexisting, before I reached over to run my hand over his back. I let it move along his shoulders and down his spine, wondering if I could melt away the tension that had settled there.

"Thank you," I finally said, when I thought I might be able to get away with saying something at all.

He whipped toward me, and I was struck by the structure of his face; how in a different life he would have been conventionally handsome instead of hard and scarred. "The way he touched you! The things he suggested. *Christo*, I should have done a hell of a lot more to him, no matter what it might have cost me."

He growled like an animal, his eyes flashing with anger.

"Stop," I said, running my hand up the back of his head, my fingers tangling in his hair. "It's nothing."

He let me touch him, and when I took his chin in my hand and turned his face toward mine, he didn't object.

My thumb traced the line of his jaw and over the soft expanse of his lips. Rio had fire in his body, and if it didn't come out as anger, perhaps I could draw it out another way.

I leaned in, tentatively, and kissed him.

His response was urgent, full of need, so fierce that it gave me shivers. I could do this to him—quell his rage, turn it into passion. When he pushed me back onto the bed, I lay back eagerly, enthusiastic to experience its depths.

His hands slid up my shirt, pulling the cotton over my head and tossing it toward the table in the corner. His fingers slid down my abdomen, leaving my skin tingling in his wake. Rio paused just long enough to reach behind my back and unsnap my bra, kissing passionately at my throat.

I tipped my head back, reveling in the feel of him, in the sharp sting of his lips upon my flesh at the rough, eager kisses. Everything was amplified—that heady scent of iron, on his palms, from this morning's workout at the gym. That rasp of his whiskers on my skin, and the scraping sound they made when he brushed against me. I let my own hands move under his shirt. I didn't have the patience or finesse he had, but I pulled the t-shirt over his head and flung it in the same direction he had sent mine.

It wasn't dark yet, afternoon light still filtering in through the window as evening began to set. Amber droplets of sweat glistened on his skin, and silky shadows traced across his body. His muscles rippled as he moved over and against me.

When he reached for my skirt I didn't stop him, and when I reached for his jeans, he allowed me to slip the button through its hole and push the denim over his hips.

Free of our clothes, his kisses continued down the length of my body, one hand sliding along the outside of my thigh. He pulled me closer until I cradled him. His touch was gentle, surprisingly sweet, though I felt a trembling beneath it, as if the gentleness was only through force of will.

Rio tugged my underwear down over my hips before stretching out on the bed beside me, his hands continuing their slow exploration and tender caress.

I moaned into his skin, arching up against his hands. Everything about his touch was electric. It had me burning, and when his hand brushed up against my center a shudder of pleasure pulsed through me.

I rocked against him as his fingers set into a rhythm, moving against me and sliding into me, until I was aching to be filled. My hips ground into his hard member, signaling with my body that I wanted more. But his hands just kept going. They flicked against me, possessing my body in rough movements that sent exquisite pleasure zigzagging down my limbs.

I gasped at the first distant warnings of orgasm on the horizon, and climbed atop him, breathing hard. *I needed him inside me.* When I screamed his name, I wanted it to be because he filled me to the brim.

But he didn't understand. He seized my shoulders and rolled me onto my back instead, sliding down to bite at my breasts, then kiss my stomach, and probe with his tongue between my legs.

Waves of pleasure spread through me again at his touch, the actions of his tongue sending delicious shivers running through me. The orgasm on the horizon—that storm that would soon break—grew closer. I pulled him back up, my hands in his hair. I wanted *him,* not his tongue. I wanted to feel his thickness within me.

I reached down, cradling his member with my hands, caressing it in long strokes. He was hard—huge and trembling, and it was obvious that he wanted this too. I kissed him fiercely, pulling him toward me, legs spreading to position him at my entrance.

Above me, he closed his eyes, his shoulders tense. *Then he pulled away from me once more.*

"Please, Rio," I said, and I almost didn't recognize my own voice, ragged with need and want. "I want you." I shouldn't have said it so plainly, maybe. There were a hundred etiquette books out there about playing hard to get that would tell me I was doing it wrong. But in that moment, I couldn't say anything else.

His only response was a growl.

I brushed my hand along the hard length of him, though I wasn't sure if it was with encouragement or frustration. "I want *this*, inside me."

Abruptly, he pulled away. "I… it's not a good idea," he said. He rolled over to show me his back.

His rejection left me bereft. That storm that had been on the horizon? It was an instant, distant memory. "You don't want me?" I said, confused. His back was… tense, every muscle rigid and outlined. When I placed my hand upon it, it was like trying to massage hard rock.

He shook his head. "I do."

My fingers ran up the rock to his shoulders, then his chin. Gently, I pulled him around to look at me. "Then what?" Only then did I notice his eyes—the emotion churning within them, looking for release.

"I… before," he started.

I waited for him to continue. He tried again. "Before—I was so angry." His hand reached out tentatively to run up my thigh. "Now, I'm not."

I knew he wasn't finished. I waited patiently.

"But… it's still there, beneath the surface. I can feel it." He took a deep breath, and I realized that some of that emotion churning in his eyes was desire, but some was also worry. "I'm… afraid of what might happen, if I let myself go. I don't want to hurt you."

My hand cupped his chin, my thumb running along that scar. "You won't. I trust you."

"I don't trust myself. I would be… rough."

I leaned in to kiss him softly on the lips, moving toward him. My cooling skin met his hot body, and my nipples hardened. "Maybe I'd like that," I whispered.

The look that crossed his eyes sent twin shivers of fear and delight skipping across my skin. He caught my mouth in a searing hot kiss. "Are you sure?"

I nodded, biting my lip. I'd never been surer of anything in my life. *I wanted to be taken. Ravished.* I wanted to be shown how much he loved me in every hard, hot thrust. "Take me," I whispered. The storm of pleasure was back on the horizon. And it was growing larger. Bolder. Threatening to be something bigger than I'd ever felt before.

He growled, and then he was upon me, pinning me on my back, one huge hand upon my shoulder as the other positioned himself. The speed with which he'd moved stunned me. I gave a gasp as he pressed against my entrance.

Then he thrust inside.

No delays, no gentle presses to tease me at my edges. One moment he was above me, and the next he was deep within me. My eyes widened as I let out a delighted gasp. A moment of pain as I stretched to take him, replaced by instant pleasure as I registered what was inside. He looked to me, giving me one last chance to shake my head and change my mind, but I nodded, instead. *I wanted this*. I wanted him to use my body for his pleasure, to take me like the whirlwind he promised and throw me from side to side. This time, I didn't want him to be gentle. I wanted him to use up his anger upon me in hard thrusts and heavy breathing and lightning that would take us both. *To show me his animal side*.

He growled, sinking down to kiss me, pressing into me. And then he began to thrust. *Oh God*. I rocked back on the bed, again and again, eventually having to lift both hands above my head to brace myself against the wall. His hard, quick pounding made my head spin and my breath quicken.

Those gray eyes were more beast than human; his face, something primal. I was a plaything to him, a ragdoll in his hands.

The thought sent thrills zinging through me almost as great as those driving between my legs. I'd never done *anything* like this. And already I knew I wanted to do it again.

I began to grind against him, matching his hard thrusts with urgent responses of my own. A hand left the wall, and I raked it in sharp tears down his ripped, muscled back. His eyes widened as a low growl rumbled from my throat — a primordial cry of pleasure to match his own. When the storm hit, it would be hard, and fast.

I moaned as every inch of him filled me. Our breaths came in short, hot, tandem bursts. I cried out his name. He rumbled a message of want and need in return.

Then suddenly he was lifting me, cradling me like I weighed nothing, one hand on my hips and one behind my shoulders. He didn't stop, and I cried out again. A ragdoll truly. I might as well try to resist this as attempt to quell a whirlwind. The thrill of his unstoppable strength electrified me with possibility.

He threw me up against the wall, the cold rock on my back a delicious counterpoint to his hot body. But my feet didn't touch the ground. Instead, they wrapped around him, gripping him, riding him. My arms curled around his neck. My hands gripped his shaggy mane of hair.

With the change in positions came a round of new sensations. Our hips slapping together as he thrust in and out. That lightning on the horizon, it was getting closer, now. I could see it in the distance, a huge mass of roiling pleasure aimed directly at me. My skin began to tingle. I could feel electricity in the air. I cried out his name as he seized me by the neck and used the leverage to drive himself again and again into my body.

His eyes were wild now, as uncontrollable as the storm. He was expending his fury in pleasure upon my body. *And I loved it.*

I loved the adrenaline which spiked my pleasure higher. I loved the desire—raw need—behind every furious breath. I loved the feeling of completely trusting someone, and having him trust me in return. I'd given my body to him. He'd revealed his weakness.

He would have his way with me. *And it thrilled me.* Because he gave me those storm clouds, almost here now, in return.

"Take me hard," I groaned. "Fuck me. *Be the beast I need you to be.*"

A snarl left his throat. I cried out as he began to swell. Over and over he slammed into me as his member engorged, pressing against me, bringing with it the storm. His head snapped back in a howl that filled the heavens. And then he was clutching me, roaring, as lightning filled both our bodies.

The storm hit like a cyclone, stripping me of reason and sanity and reprieve. I cried out, barely conscious of my voice, as explosions racked me repeatedly, each one larger than the last—chain lightning that forked through me in time to the hard jolts of his hot member.

The lightning didn't stop until his head was slumped against the wall. He let me slide slowly down to my feet. I stayed that way, gasping, using him as support as I swayed from side to side.

He nuzzled my neck, and I closed my eyes, enjoying the delicious tickle. "You have to get angry more often," I whispered with a grin.

He pulled back and I searched his face. The anger was gone—not a trace remained in his eyes. Instead, there was calm. Pure, joyous, exhausted calm. He smiled, caressing me tenderly. "I've been angry all my life, Bella. The great sex? With you, that's easy. But the anger? That's getting harder and harder to sustain."

17: RIO

I'd always been a light sleeper, but having Bella in my arms was almost soporific—her body held the nightmares at bay. I didn't dream of bloodied figures on a cold marble floor. I didn't dream of smoking guns and horrible betrayal. For just the briefest moment in time, I forgot why I was here, in this hellhole, and was just a man once more.

The sound of Lumen's voice hummed on the edge of my consciousness, and for a moment, in my drowsy state, I wondered at the new dream I was having. It wasn't until the pounding at the door began that I started, fully awake.

Lumen banged on my door and called my name— loudly, again. If he'd had any intentions of being discreet, they had apparently disappeared with my inability to wake in a timely matter.

I snatched for my jeans, still buttoning them up when I flung the door open.

"Christo!" I snapped. The light filtering in through the balcony was still pale. It was barely morning, and Lumen had a wild, frantic look about him that did little to settle my unease. "What is it?"

He tossed a look over his shoulder, down the stairwell, before stepping into the room.

Out of the corner of my eye, I saw Bella sit up in bed, clutching the thin sheet to her body.

"Rio," Lumen began, clearly agitated. "You know how you told me to keep an eye on things for you?"

I nodded.

"The guards are looking for Bella."

I looked toward Bella, her beautiful body still clothed in bedsheets, as a grin broke out upon her face. "Rio, it worked!"

Though the thought of her leaving tore at something deep inside me, I forced a smile. "That's great news. The best."

Lumen grabbed my arm. "Rio, you don't understand! They're looking for her. And you!"

I stilled. "Why would they be looking for me?"

"The Razors—you know how they have pull with the guards. They've put out a rumor that you kidnapped her, it's the reason she's still in the prison."

Rage flared within me, absent one minute, all-consuming the next. The incident in the courtyard, and now this—they had no intention of keeping the truce. All they wanted was to bring me down. The Red blanketed my vision, coating everything the color of blood. "I'll kill every one of them," I grated.

Lumen's hand was still on my arm. He tugged at it urgently. "Rio, you have to listen. They'll kill you."

I was not new to this place or its ways, and the incident from the other day was still fresh in my mind, those rosary beads swaying on the door. But I didn't care. That someone would suggest I was intentionally hurting Bella—the thought made my blood boil inside.

But then the sheets rustled behind me, and Bella's hand was beside Lumen's, a blanket wrapped around her body. "Rio, please. Your anger can't help, here. But you can."

How did I tell her all the things that were going on inside me? I'd finally found someone—someone who understood me. Someone who made me want to be a better person. Someone who made this life in prison bearable— no, worse, someone without whom life in prison would now be unbearable?

I looked at her, and opened my mouth to say these things, and realized I couldn't. She wasn't made for prison, this beautiful flower. What I felt didn't matter. The only thing that mattered was seeing her out of this shithole safe and sound.

I nodded, some small part of me looking on in detached amazement at the sudden absence of rage in my body. At the sudden absence of *anything*. "It's time. Get dressed, quickly now."

Lumen turned as she picked up her clothes. *I didn't.*

I knew I should—I knew it was indecent, but my eyes wouldn't let me. She dropped the sheet, dressing, and I drank her in, a man on the edge of a desert, taking one last glass of water.

"Come now," Lumen said, when she was done. He reached for her arm and pulled her through the doorway. "We'll get you to the guards."

She only realized I wasn't coming when she turned, to find me still standing inside the room. She pulled against Lumen's arm as he tugged her out the doorway. "Rio?"

I shook my head. "I'll meet you there."

We both knew it was a lie.

"Rio?" Her voice had an edge of hysteria to it. "I'll tell the guards. It will be fine."

I shook my head. It wouldn't work. The guards had been looking for an excuse to hang me for as long as I'd been here. And though I didn't care about that—not any

113

more—I did care about Bella getting caught in the crossfire. Because I wouldn't go down easily, and when the time came, that meant I didn't want Bella nearby.

I yanked a hand through my hair, still tempted to follow. If I had to be without her, in a shithole like el Castillo, did it really matter if I was dead or alive?

The short answer was no. The more complicated answer was, I wanted whatever was best for Bella.

18: BELLA

Skirt held up with one hand so I didn't trip, I hurried down the hall next to Lumen.

I barely knew him—had only just met him, but I clung to him like a lifeline.

The prison was enormous, much larger than the small area that I'd seen in my time here. We crossed corridors, rooms stinking of garbage and effluence, even one or two courtyards smaller than the main one, but still full of sunlight. I had thought the layout of the prison was straightforward, but apparently, we'd only stuck to territory under Rio's control.

We came to a set of stairs I hadn't seen before. Lumen waved impatiently at me to get down them, concern etched on his face, though I wasn't sure if it was because of the rumors the Razors had spread, or something else. He would take me to the warden's office; he'd said when we started. Once I was close, he would leave me to walk the last bit of distance myself.

Those rumors must be bad, then. I thought again of the rosary beads that counted down a man's final days. Surely they wouldn't hand them out on the strength of a rumor?

The guards looking for me should have been a good thing. It meant that my father had received my letter, and that my time here was over. But if that was the case, why did I feel the urge to hide, now, instead of escaping? If I left, what would happen to Lumen? And Rio?

My night with Rio still lingered fresh on my mind—his hands, trembling in their intensity, rough upon my skin. My thighs still ached from our lovemaking. Each step I took was a reminder of exactly how much I had enjoyed my time with him. The sweet throb became almost hypnotic—the tender muscles a reminder of what had been, an echo of Rio to keep me company.

And then we stopped.

I looked up to find five guards filling the narrow corridor, dressed in riot gear. One of them paused in the act of pushing a prostitute against a wall, a photograph held in her face. He let her go when he saw me, and the woman backed away, giving me nervous glances as she rubbed at her neck.

"Well, well, well," he growled. "It seems like you've saved us the trouble of hunting you down."

Another grabbed Lumen, who had held up his hands in a gesture of peace. "Don't worry Miss, you're safe now," the guard said. A fist slammed suddenly into Lumen's face, knocking him against the wall. "This man can't hurt you anymore."

I was stupid. My hand went to my mouth in shock, instead of screaming at them to stop. By the time words had formed, Lumen was being pummeled by batons and fists.

"No! Stop!" I finally managed.

I slammed my fists ineffectually against the guards until I could interrupt their focus. They let Lumen fall to the ground in a crumpled ball, gasping for breath and moaning.

"Isabella Martin?" one of the guards demanded.

I nodded my head, though I wasn't sure if I was about to be treated the same way.

"This fiend," said the same guard, gesturing to Lumen on the ground. "He is responsible for trapping you here in the prison, holding you against your will?"

My eyes widened. The claim was so far from the truth that it beggared belief. I'd been so foolish, to think that the Razors would slink away and not get their revenge. *Maybe I should have let Rio have his way with them after all.*

I shook my head, thinking quickly. "That's not what happened. He's just a boy I asked for directions. I don't even know him. I don't know his name or why he's here. He was just doing me a favor."

The guard frowned. My explanation was far from satisfactory.

"No one trapped me in here or kept me against my will," I muttered. "I mean, no one other than the guards and they were just doing their job. I just... wandered in by accident," I said lamely. "I... I thought they did tours." Even to my own mind, the idea now seemed stupid.

"You will come with us," the guard said. They formed a box around me—as if I needed to be kept safe. I was marched off, and could only twist around and glance through them once to see Lumen, still in a crumpled heap upon the floor.

***

The sudden silence jarred me. The room I'd been taken to—past prison tenements, through a secure door, and then along neat white corridors that smelled of antiseptic and money—was devoid of personality.

I wanted to walk the space. I wanted to see if there were any clues on the other side of the desk that dominated the room about what would happen next; anything that might help me have a better idea of what I could expect.

But instead, I sat in the chair, my legs pulled up, my arms hugging them to my chest, and thought over and over about Rio, and Lumen with his bloodied face. The boy wasn't dead—his chest had risen and fallen. But he might well soon be. The sudden violence of the guards terrified me more than anything the Razors had ever done, even more than the riot. Because this violence had been done so casually. It hadn't been passionate. It hadn't even been premediated. It had meant as little to the guard as throwing out the trash. And it spoke volumes of his opinion of the people under him. Lumen had known not to fight back. And that in turn told me even more—things like this had happened more than once.

The minutes ticked by. My misery deepened.

And then the door flung open, and my father stepped into the room.

"Bella!" he cried, flinging his arms open and moving quickly toward me. He pulled me to my feet, pausing to take my face in his hands and twist it this way and that, as though trying to convince himself I was still in one piece. He pulled me into a brief hug. "I have been so worried. Working night and day to discover where you disappeared to."

I blushed. My poor father. For a moment, my worry for Rio was eclipsed by an immense feeling of stupidity. What had I been thinking running off like that? I'd been so innocent.

The sound of a throat clearing interrupted our reunion. Gateau materialized from behind my father. "Bella, I'm so glad you are safe," he murmured.

I looked at him, confused. "What are you doing here?"

"Gateau was instrumental in finding you," my father answered. "Did you know he has contacts inside the prison?"

He demurred with a shake of his head. "I keep my ears open, that is all. I'm just glad you're safe."

"I should have thought to check here sooner," my father continued. "It never occurred to me you might be trapped here."

"It's okay, Papa," I said, suddenly more tired than I could have imagined. The whole thing seemed impossible now, and soon I would take my leave of this place — forever.

Gateau strode toward the guard. "*Señor*, you have my word that the guards will be punished harshly for their negligence with this woman. I am appalled that Bella had to spend her time with these criminals. I can only imagine how damaging that must have been for her, how frightened she was."

"I'm fine," I protested.

Gateau shook his head. "They're scum, Bella. The lowest of the low. I'll have the men who kept you here shot for what they did."

I shook my head. Once the words would have shocked me. But now… "One's in a coma. The other's already dead."

He smiled grimly. "Then I'll take it out on someone else. Bella, I have some small amount of sway here — not much, but I can pull some strings. Tell me who it was that kidnapped you, and I'll see the Rosary hanging on his door by sundown."

I went pale at just the thought. If I'd eaten breakfast, I would have thrown it up. "I came here on my own."

"That's not what my contacts have said. They said you were in the company of a huge, tattooed villain. One of the worst, I'm told."

"Then your contacts are liars." I wanted to kick Gateau—to claw him, to tear his eyes out for what he was suggesting.

He shook his head. "The guards confirmed it—the man they found you with is a known accomplice."

My father watched the exchange between us like a tennis match, his head going back and forth with each new piece of conversation. He stepped forward now, though. "Bella, you're confused. And I'm sure Gateau won't lay charges, if I don't want him to. I'll take you from this town. We will leave and return to America—this isn't the place for you."

"Stop, Papa. It's fine. *I* am fine. I didn't hate it. I mean, I hated some of it. I hated the prison. I hated these walls. But the people... there are good people in there, struggling to survive."

They looked at me as if I were a pathetic creature bereft of her wits. It sent boiling heat down my veins. "There are children here, Papa. Children whose only crime is having been born to a mother and father who could not pay their way out of trouble."

"You cannot explain away the crimes of every single individual in this building. It's a prison, for God's sake."

"Would you rather them all be orphans?" Gateau added. "Little street rats that pawed at scraps outside the walls?"

"Orphans," I said, turning on him. "You hit the nail on the head. There are people dying in here for the Warden's profit." I turned to my father, noting the pale purple color blooming under his skin. *He loved me, but he didn't believe me.*

"Bella, this conversation is over."

I shook my head, trying to suppress the tremble that was taking over my body. I couldn't leave, not like this. Those children in the courtyard? First it was their teacher that disappeared. How long until it was their parents?

Gateau smiled grimly. "She's obviously affected," he said to my father. He spoke as if I wasn't even in the room. "I've heard of this. Stockholm Syndrome."

"Is it bad?" My father spoke as if I wasn't there either.

Gateau nodded. "It can be. I mean look at her! She's talking about people going missing and the Warden being evil! But don't worry. As soon as she's out, I'll see her attackers brought to justice."

His words filled me with terror. He was talking about Rio. A horrible, overwhelming *uselessness* overcame me. In prison, I'd been someone. But out here? I was just a daughter to be ignored. There was nothing I could do, from the outside. The situation was hopeless.

But only from the outside.

A shiver ran through me as a wild, crazy thought started to blossom. There was one thing I could do. One thing to ensure that I captured my father's attention. One thing that would make him look at the conditions in this hellhole and fight to ensure they were fixed.

If his daughter was the one suffering them. If I stayed on the inside, instead of walking out into the light.

"I'm not leaving," I said quietly. Rio was the one who had said it—*sometimes, you had to stand up for what was right.*

All motion in the room ground to a halt.

"What?"

I crossed my arms over my chest. "I said, I'm not leaving." Once I started talking it was impossible to stop. "Maybe if your daughter is trapped inside, Papa, you'll pay attention to the conditions she must face."

"This is really not something I can condone," Gateau began stiffly.

"I don't care!" I cried. "All I care about is making things better! There are people in this prison. Human beings! And they're being treated like animals."

Gateau's eyes narrowed into dangerous slits. "I'm sure the Warden is treating them fairly."

121

I stomped over to the door. "And that's exactly why I'm staying inside." I pulled it open and shouted at the guards.

They jumped, surprised to see a prisoner beckoning them, and pushed into the room. "Is there a problem here?" one asked.

"Yes, there's a problem," I answered. "I don't know these men. Take me back."

"Bella-" my father started. Gateau rumbled something about me being absurd.

"Shut up," I said, my voice cracking like a whip. "Both of you. Until you find a way to bring justice back to this place, I will not step a foot outside of these walls."

I turned to the guards once more. "I've told you I'm the wrong person. Letting me go with these men is tantamount to letting me escape." My head snaked toward my father. "I'm certainly no daughter of a man that would let an atrocity like this remain in the middle of his city."

The guards traded confused questions with my father, while Gateau glared at me. I smiled in triumph, my heart pounding, my ears humming with the adrenaline coursing through my body. "Take me back," I demanded of the guards.

My father began to protest. At a word from Gateau, the guards blocked the door and did not move.

He smiled, a puckered slit on his pallid flesh. "You darling little child," he said. "It doesn't work that way. You have not committed a crime, therefore you have no right to call yourself a prisoner."

His grin was like a torch, flaring every nerve in my body into angry heat. I'd taught Rio how to be calm. But it seemed Rio had taught me something in return. "You know what, Gateau? You're absolutely right." *Sometimes, you needed to fight.*

The guard didn't see it coming. My punch was sharp, a clean right uppercut that sent him staggering into the wall.

That one was to get me out of here. I leapt at him, punching him again. *And that, was for Lumen*.

The voices in the room turned to a roar as I let loose on the man's face. I heard it only dimly. All the insults, the loathsome hypocrisy of the place—it was pain between my knuckles; distilled vengeance, action that made things right. The more my fists hurt, the more pain I was inflicting on the bastards who let this place fester into what it had become. I understood Rio, for the first time—all that anger and pain. It made me strong, too. It was what I needed, in this moment, to get where I needed to be.

They pulled me away and the noise came back. Father was screaming as a guard held him from me. Gateau said nothing, just watched as the other two dragged me away. I looked at the man on the floor. He moaned and rolled onto his side. His face was purpled and already swelling in patches. I kicked him as they dragged me past, a furious, crazed grin splitting my face.

19: RIO

She burst into my room like a mountain wildcat. When I was a child the *gata salvaje* sometimes came down from the mountains, untamed and angry, confused at where they were and scratching anyone that came close. I did now what I'd done then—approached cautiously, with soothing words. Sometimes, but not always, you could calm them if you knew the trick.

"Bella?"

The noise from her throat reminded me again of a wildcat—a high pitched yowl that was half fury, half desperate confusion.

"Bella. It's okay. Whatever it is."

With wildcats, you had to be careful. If you didn't approach them with meat, they'd go for you, snapping and snarling as they tried to rip off your hand. Here, all I had was myself. I opened my arms, gesturing for her. "I'm here."

She rushed forward with a sob. "Rio!"

"It's okay," I whispered, stroking her hair. It still smelled faintly of sunshine and Jasmine, the perfume wafting at me as I held her close. "Whatever it is, it's okay."

She didn't answer, her shoulders heaving in my arms. When she wiped at her cheeks there was blood on her knuckles.

"Shouldn't you be home, by now?" I finally ventured, when I thought that she could talk. She growled again, but a different growl, which said her anger had passed. I fought the urge to chuckle. My wildcat. *My gata salvaje.*

"I refused to leave." She said the words with finality, like it wouldn't matter what I had to say about it or how I felt.

My hand paused mid-stroke. Refused to leave? I wanted to ask her more, but I didn't. She needed me, right now, as the anger left her. I knew, from experience, that the emotion would leave her exhausted. Everything else, she could tell me in her own time.

Her body settled into mine. "Thank you for holding me."

"Thank you for coming back, I guess. What on earth were you thinking, refusing to leave?"

She looked up at me, her eyes still red, but burst out laughing. "I kind of got… angry. You've rubbed off on me, I think."

I rolled my eyes. "Well you're a bigger fool than I thought. The only good thing about being angry is the sex."

She blushed, at that, and bit her lip. "It was pretty good. Maybe that's why I came back."

I raised an eyebrow, but didn't say a word. Eventually the smile faltered, and the entire ordeal came out. Lumen, her father, the guards and what they'd said they'd do. By the end, I wasn't sure if I was holding her or she was holding me back. The only thing that stopped the Red flooding through me was the knowledge that I couldn't afford to lose control—not while Bella needed me. Not while I held her in my arms.

As if sensing the tension in my muscles, her arms locked around me tighter. "Please Rio. Don't do anything stupid. They said some bad things—things I didn't think should happen, that's all. Papa will fix it, now that he knows I'm here. Things will change."

***

I waited on edge for them to come back for Bella—to demand that she leave the prison with them. It's what I would have done, in my rage and fury.

But they did not come.

As the time passed—hours, and then days—and the knot of anticipation in the pit of my stomach loosened, it became easier to believe that things would go back to being the way they had been—a parody of idyllic life. Late nights exploring her body and bringing her to completion, sleepy mornings filled with contentment instead of reality. If I could go on like that forever, I'd be the first to suggest we had no need for change.

On her tenth morning in prison, and her fifth since walking back in, we were up with the sun and Bella ran a brush through her hair—one I'd managed to coax from a Razor girl with trinkets and a dollop of liquor—plaiting it into a thick braid that hung down her back. She smoothed the front of her skirt before pressing a kiss to my scarred cheek.

We didn't talk about where the other teacher had gone or why she hadn't returned. But spending her days with the children had become her routine.

I had my own routine. I'd lie in bed, the sheets pulled just over my hips, or tangled around my thighs, and we'd talk as she got dressed. I'd stay that way as she left, catching her kisses as she walked out the door, but as soon as she disappeared I'd leap up, moving to the window, and hold my breath until I saw her again.

There were so many reasons why I shouldn't let her go down into the courtyard alone—the Razors might break their truce; her father might bribe the guards to take her out by force. But all of them faded to nothing before her smile. She wanted to help the children, and that was that. I couldn't be with her every second of every day, so either I banned her from going at all, or I accepted it as a risk she was willing to take, and tried to do the same.

She always came back. At the end of the day, after teaching them the alphabet, or playing tag, or on one memorable afternoon where Mateo had taught the class Morse Code, she would always return, appearing in my doorway like she belonged there. And she did. I didn't think of the room as mine alone anymore. It was ours. I'd picked up another toothbrush and managed to trade for a new blouse and skirt for Bella. It had cost me goods and more bottled water than was wise, but it was worth it to see her smile.

In the cover of the night I would slip off her clothing and enjoy the feeling of her body wrapped in mine. The darkness stopped me from seeing her smile, but I could still feel it, and hear it. And the beauty of it never got old.

At times, she would inquire about my past—about the missing tattoo, and why I was in prison—but I always deflected it away. I considered, from time to time, telling her the truth about Elizabeth and the bank robbery. I thought of all the ways I could explain what happened. But every time I practiced the story in my mind, it ended with me talking about a life I'd led with another woman. And every time I imagined how that conversation would go, my imaginary Bella walked away. So I became used to the rhythm of our days, and the pleasantness of keeping that secret to myself.

On the tenth day, though, the routine changed. Bella was running the brush though her hair, planting a kiss on my cheek, when noise echoed up from the courtyard. The ring of a hammer striking nail sent an instant spike of dread through my body, freezing me, stopping me too late from preventing Bella moving to the window. "Bella, don't..." My voice trailed off as her face paled in the weak morning light.

My heart broke as I watched her reaction, and I moved quickly to her side. "Don't look, *gata salvaje*," I said, wrapping my arms around her. She couldn't have known the condemned man's week was up, or that the execution would happen in such a public, prominent place. The gallows stood today where she had played with the children yesterday.

"Is that what I think it is?" Bella asked.

I nodded. There would be no children in the courtyard today. No adult prisoners, either, bar one. In a place where children played, a grown man would die; the timber gallows a Lego platform used so often that they kept the pre-drilled boards in storage. It made it easier to bolt together in the early morning light.

"When did they do this?"

They were almost finished—the platform erected, the final nails now hammered into place. "The guards build quickly. They are very efficient, now." With the sun rising, the courtyard was eerily silent, as though it, too, were appalled by how cheap life was inside.

It was a public display by the Warden, meant to cow the inmates. And it did, though we resisted in our own little way. People would watch from the windows, but they wouldn't attend. Not in person. A man would die for our overlord's pleasure. We'd keep vigil, but wouldn't condone.

We would come, instead, in the night, when they had taken him down—the body left on display. The widow, first, if there was one. Then the family and friends, trickling in twos and threes. After that the gang leaders, all debts and feuds forgotten. In our hatred of the Warden, we stood united. Last of all, the community would let in the children. *In el Castillo, you grew up fast.*

She shivered, wrapping her arms around herself, but refused to be pulled away from the window. "Why do they do this in public," she asked. "It's barbaric."

"As a reminder that we were all under el Castillo's thumb—that our lives no longer belong to us."

She settled against my chest, both of us drawn in by the gallows below. The noose that hung from the end swung like a pendulum in the faint, cold morning breeze.

"It's… it's like we live in a glass house," she whispered. "No one deserves this."

I didn't respond. All I could think was that she'd just said *we.*

They brought the prisoner out shortly. I turned from the window, then, unwilling to watch what came next. He was sobbing, calling out to a god who didn't care, or in the shadows of the prison, just didn't see.

I had seen enough death—enough loss. I didn't need to see any more. There was no god in this prison but the Warden himself.

Bella lingered in the shadows, fidgeting in and out of the window's edge.

A pang of sympathy speared my heart for her. I had been there too, at the shadow's edge, the first time I had seen an execution. "No one will stop it."

"What?" Bella asked, startled. She looked at me as if I'd read her mind.

"In case that's what you're waiting for. No one is going to save him."

"How do you know that's what I was waiting for?"

I sat down on the cot, closing my eyes, my shoulders heavy. "Because it's what I was waiting for, the first time." I

129

watched two or three before I realized it would never happen. Seeing Bella at that window… the pain was just as fresh, today.

I stared at the floor, dreading and anticipating what would come next. I could follow the process without watching; there was no window to close, or sound system to turn up. I might cover my ears, perhaps, but I wouldn't. It just never felt right.

They announced his name and punishment—Bella looking on from the window, myself sitting still upon the bed, and I held my breath. It was like the entire world had stopped, for this one moment in time. Nobody moved—not in the courtyard, not at the windows. There were no distant clinks from the gym, or catcalls between far-off buildings. Even the prostitutes and drug dealers would give a moment's silence, though they would both do a roaring trade tonight.

I had so much power here in prison, but when it all came down to it, I had nothing. That could have been my worst enemy on that platform, or my dearest friend—it made no difference, in the end. I was a king among my people, but the kingdom was one of insects. We might scurry here and there behind walls and in dark corners, playing at politics, but even the greatest among us could do nothing against the Warden's boot. It came down where he pleased, and all the power in the world would do nothing to stop it.

The thump of feet rang loud on the wooden platform. Final words were said, too distant to make out. And then the silence that always preceded the fall.

The only sound at the fall was the gasp from Bella.

"That's it then," I said, standing. I moved to Bella, who still stood with her hand over her mouth. I could do nothing to stop the death, but I could help Bella. She'd need me, now. She had a glazed look in her eyes; she stared but did not see. I wondered if she regretted choosing prison over her freedom. "They'll leave the body on the platform, tonight, we will pay our respects-"

I paused. Two guards were holding a stretcher. They rolled the body onto it, then took it away.

That wasn't part of the protocol. Not even close.

"Do you think it's true?" Bella asked, beside me. "About the organs? Would they really take healthy people and find a reason to kill them?"

I stared down at the empty platform. Did I believe it could be happening? *Absolutely.*

Did I think that the men who ran the prison were coldhearted enough to make a profit from our freshly executed bodies? *I didn't even have to think twice.*

I pulled her in toward me. "There's nothing we can do, Bella, even if it is."

She whirled toward me, brushing off my hand and poking me in the chest with her forefinger. "I came back because this place needed change, and I'd have a better voice from inside the walls. If I'm not going to do anything while I'm here to make it better, then I'm just wasting everyone's time. Mine. Yours. The children's." She took a deep breath that was half sob. "The killings, the drugs, the prostitutes, this whole system is *corrupt*, Rio!"

"I know," I said quietly. "I live here."

Immediately, she softened. "I'm sorry. I didn't mean it like that. I've been here less than two weeks. I can't imagine what it must be like for you."

Insects, before the boot. If I thought about it too much, it would overwhelm me. "I survive. It's the only thing I can do."

"There has to be more to it than that."

I shook my head, my only answer. I could rule the inmates, but not the guards. If they ever came for Mateo, or Lumen, or Bella? I would fight, I knew that. And I also knew that in the end, it wouldn't change anything. No matter how many of them I took down before I died, they'd still get their way in the end. Even the entire prison together couldn't beat the guards behind their thick, high walls. I wanted to rage at the helplessness, but the emotion was like pounding my fists in the ocean and watching them get swallowed. It achieved no purpose. I couldn't even make a splash.

Bella, it seemed, had her own set of thoughts to wrestle with. "I'm going for a walk," she said simply. "I'd like to be alone for a while."

I pretended not to see the tear that slid delicately down one beautiful cheek. She was too soft for this life, my Bella.

Let her have her walk. When she got back, I would end this foolishness, and make her leave the jail. The fact that my heart would break when she did was no longer important.

20: BELLA

I couldn't go back to him. Not yet.

I was angry and I didn't know why, confused but I didn't know what about. We'd just seen someone die. *Die!* And yet Rio had done... nothing. Every time there'd been trouble, he'd fixed it. Every time something went wrong, he'd had a plan. I wanted to be mad at him for his inaction at the execution. To be furious at this huge man who could solve so many things with his bulk and his energy, with his tattoos and his street smarts, but who'd merely sat on his bed and let this happen.

But I knew that wasn't fair. He'd sat with his head in his hands, shoulders slumped, helpless, through the entire thing. I'd never seen him like that. *Defeated*. And it made me so angry, but I didn't know why. And it made me confused, but I didn't know what about.

So, I walked.

I walked through empty corridors, and an empty gym. The cafeteria was silent. The air was silent too.

I almost walked past Ezzi, as my eyes stared sightlessly ahead. I only looked up at the sound of her rapid breathing. She leaned against a wall, eyes to the floor. No, she wasn't leaning—she was holding herself up.

"Ezzi," I said. "It's Bella. Are you alright?"

As she looked at me, I knew immediately that she was not.

Before, I had thought she was young, just a girl. Now, as I stared into her unfocused eyes, she was much older than I had realized. Still beautiful, in her way, but not that girlish wisp I had thought she'd been. She was high, or perhaps coming down from a drug, but her beauty was something that survived despite what she did to herself. It sat in the lines around her eyes, and the cracks in her cheap makeup. It fell in the curl of her dark hair.

She fidgeted at the fabric of her pretty dress as she focused on me, eyes slightly glazed. *Rio had said the Razors hooked their prostitutes with cocaine.*

For just a moment I was overwhelmed by the whole thing—the thought of Mateo and the nights he must have witnessed, and the highs and lows of a mother trapped in a never-ending cycle. People in el Castillo died daily in more ways than just one.

"Hey," I said softly. I took her hands. They trembled. "Where's Mateo?"

"He's fine," she said. She looked around, as if she had misplaced him somewhere nearby, before shaking off her confusion, and granting me a smile. "He's with friends." Her profile caught the light, revealing a red angry mark over one cheek.

"Did the Razors do that to you," I asked.

"No," she said. "Just a creep. Over and done with now."

"You poor thing."

She gave a laugh—it was pretty and musical, and yet somehow still sent shivers down my spine. There was an edge to the laugh that was... desperate. The laugh stopped abruptly. "I guess that's why I should stick with the Razors, isn't it? Safety in numbers. Not all of us have someone like el Lobo to protect us."

"Ezzi, I-"

Her face suddenly darkened with worry. She looked around the hall, frantic. "Where's Mateo?"

She was drug addled. Didn't know what she was saying.

"Shh, it's alright," I said, grabbing her hand. "He's with friends. He's safe." I silently prayed I wasn't lying to her.

Ezzi leaned back against the wall and slid to the floor. It didn't feel right to tower over her, so I knelt at her side.

"You asked me before if I enjoyed what I do," she said suddenly. "That was you, right?"

"Yes," I said.

"I'm not enjoying it today," she said, her voice breaking.

I had no idea what to do, so I put my hand on her shoulder and squeezed it as she quietly wept for a few moments. "I'm sorry."

"No, don't be," she finally said, wiping away tears with her palm. "It's just been a bad day."

"A bad client?"

She nodded, then looked left and right down the empty corridor. "Can I tell you something?" she asked, her voice a whisper.

I leaned in. "Sure."

"The Razors bring in outsiders. New clients that don't belong here."

"You mentioned that before, the day you picked Mateo up from school." I said, frowning. I hadn't thought about it then, but now that I did... that was a little strange, wasn't it?

"They're bringing in more all the time," Ezzi continued. "So many they don't have enough girls to service them all. I ask not to work with them, but they stop the *cocaína,* if I refuse." Her hand went up to her face and she probed the tender flesh, wincing.

We sat in silence, and Ezzi began to cry once more, without moving, as though she hadn't noticed the tears falling down her cheeks. "I can't raise my son like this anymore," she said in a strange, monotone voice. My heart broke to hear it.

I took Ezzi by both hands. I couldn't stop the execution, but maybe here, in my own small way, I could do something to help. "Give up the cocaína, Ezzi. For your son," I pleaded.

She shook her head, finally noticing the tears. A dirty hand went to her cheek to wipe at them, smudging her mascara. "You don't understand. Even if I could, I wouldn't leave."

I frowned. "But they beat you. Why would you stay?"

She looked off down the corridor. When she spoke, it was to herself. "They're my family. The other girls, and the Razors." Now she did look at me. "In here, you need family. If you don't have one…" She drew a deep breath, then let it out. "At least with the Razors, I get paid when my body is used."

I thought about that first day I'd walked into prison, and shivers ran down my body. I knew exactly what she meant. I took her hand once again.

She squeezed it. "Sometimes I think you don't know how lucky you are. El Lobo doesn't allow cocaína in his quadrant. Sometimes I wish… I wish I'd made different choices. That I had a different family."

I offered her a smile, pulling out a handkerchief to dab at her mascara. "Well, maybe we could sort of be that for each other. We could have our own little family." I said the words a little too brightly, but I wasn't surprised to find I also found them appealing.

She wrinkled her nose just slightly. "Really? You think el Lobo is looking for another girl? Maybe to start his own ring?"

My jaw dropped. I forced it closed with a light laugh. "I don't think so." I dabbed at the mascara again. "What I meant was, Rio protects the people in his quadrant. You wouldn't have to work at all."

She smiled at me sadly. "He looks after Mateo, and I'm grateful. But he doesn't allow drugs in his quadrant."

"Then stop."

"It's not that simple," she said, throwing up her hands. My cloth left a long streak of mascara on her cheek. "I've tried! But each time, I break and go running back. When I'm sober, it's the only thing I can think about. Nothing else matters—not my body, not these bruises, nothing!"

"Not even your son?" I asked quietly. I held my breath, waiting for her answer.

"He's the most important thing in the world," she said, so softly I barely heard her. She looked up at me. "Am I a bad mother?"

I shook my head. "No. But your son needs you sober." I stood, pulling her to her feet. "Come on, let's get you home."

We walked in silence down the corridor. When she stumbled, I put my arm around her waist. "I'll have a word with el Lobo for you. If you promise to quit, I promise that he'll take you in."

She stiffened. "You would do that, for me?"

I nodded.

"I don't think I can go cold turkey."

"You won't. We'll slowly taper your dose. It won't be pleasant, but I'll be by your side the whole time. You can help me teach, to keep you occupied." I thought hard. I didn't want Ezzi sneaking out at night when I wasn't around. But in a prison with few doors and even fewer locks, what could I do to stop her?

The answer came to me. "And we'll have a curfew—you don't go anywhere without your son."

We arrived at her room—a single cell with a tattered sheet hanging over the doorway. It was a tiny, cramped hole, half crowded with piping that ran from floor to ceiling. When we entered, the pipes were humming—faint tings and whistles from movement far below.

"This is… nice," I said. It had the look of someone doing the best they could do with next to nothing.

"It's all I could get," Ezzi said softly. "You can't even hear the pipes after a while."

"I wonder what they're from?"

Ezzi's eyes went distant. "We're directly above the isolation cells," she answered. "It's hard to ignore the sound, when the men scream."

I sat down on the bed beside Ezzi. *Oh God*. Maybe Mateo being deaf was a blessing. Though he'd still feel the vibrations, every time he tried to sleep.

Ezzi looked at me, a terrible hope pushing through the haze of her high. "You really think el Lobo might help me? That I wouldn't have to work with the Razors? That I could move into his quadrant?"

"I do. He's fearsome, Ezzi, but he has a gentle heart." I flashed her a cheeky smile, trying to raise the mood. "And if for some reason he disagrees?" I raised an eyebrow and stuck a hand on my hip. "Let's just say we both know tricks to change a man's mind."

She giggled. "I like you, Bella."

"I like you too, Ezzi. Now I think it's time for you to sleep."

She lay down. "Stay with me a while?"

I nodded, pulling a thin blanket over her. We sat in silence for several moments, listening to the sounds of the pipes until a thought entered my mind. "Ezzi?"

"Yes?" she said sleepily.

"You said there were new faces coming to see you?"

She nodded. "Outsiders."

"How are they getting inside?"

"They wouldn't like me telling you," she said drowsily.

That meant it wasn't by the front door. I shook her lightly by the shoulder. "Don't go to sleep yet, Ezzi. This is important. Is there a way out of the prison I don't know about?"

Her eyes fluttered briefly. "Not for us. I thought that too, before…" Her eyes closed again. "I thought that too."

There was another exit! I shook her again. "You have to tell me, Ezzi."

"It's a side gate, near the Apex. The Razors control that part of the prison, and the guards let clients in for a cut. Clients in, but we're not allowed out." She repeated the phrase in a sing song tone, her voice trailing off. "Clients in, but we're not allowed..." Her last words ended in a gentle snore.

Behind me, the blanket hanging over the door rustled. I spun, but it was only Mateo, entering with a giggle.

I threw up my hands in exaggerated surprise. Mateo smiled broadly, then slipped past me to crawl into the bed with his mother. He hugged her with one arm and tucked himself into the cramped space with practiced familiarity. I pulled the cover over him too, and left.

I hurried down the hall. *A way out.* So many possibilities to consider. If I could slip out, I could get Mateo the watch battery he needed. I could reach Father again and keep pressing him for help.

I turned a corner. *No,* I thought. *Think bigger.*

If I could stake this *Apex* out, I could learn who these men were who beat women. Rio could get to them, on the inside. Or I could spread the word when I got out. Either way would stop the beatings and keep Ezzi safe.

I turned another corner. *No. Think bigger.*

There was a way out! This Apex would be less guarded than the main entrance, and they were used to men coming and going. I entered the main concourse, excited. This was my chance to help Rio escape! I turned a final corner, excited to tell him my news.

Too late I heard the noise from behind. I turned just as a baton rushed down toward me. A blanket of blackness swallowed me before I'd even hit the floor.

21: RIO

Bella was still gone when I opened my eyes the next morning.

I didn't like her being out there alone, not when so much had transpired of late. Normally, I wasn't someone that gave chase, but like it or not, concern eventually overwhelmed my stubbornness. I found myself searching for her not long after I woke.

I checked the courtyard first—the dry expanse of dirt and shadow was dotted with people in the early cool of morning, but none of them were the woman that I wanted. I checked the gym next, the scent of steel and concrete as familiar to me as the tattoos upon my own skin. Lumen was there, checking off the names of the bulked-out gangsters that used my equipment. As my second in command, he kept an eye on the place when he wasn't cooking.

He shook his head when I asked him. "I've been hearing rumors though. The Razors are angry about something."

"They're always angry."

"No, this is something new. Apparently, a *gringa* has been fucking with their product."

A shiver ran through me. *A white woman.* I thanked him and hurried away. The Razors dealt in women. What had Bella's too kind heart got her into now?

Hallways, stairwells, I even checked the women's restrooms, pushing gruffly inside to call her name. Bella was nowhere to be seen.

I was searching an ancillary courtyard when I suddenly stopped. Had she left? Had she just got up and walked out of the prison? It wouldn't be the first time it had happened.

Nightmares of Elizabeth still haunted my dreams. Of her laughing on those courtroom steps.

I shook my head. No. Bella wasn't like that. And she'd had no reason to use me, like that other woman had.

I was anxiously scanning the cafeteria when Diego found me. He approached from the side, and threw me roughly against the wall. An arm pushed against my throat. Cold metal pricked at my skin. "You owe me, *vato*."

I looked down to note a homemade shiv pressed against my side—a spoon that had been sharpened to a point. "I don't know what you're talking about." I growled and flexed, pushing up from the wall. "And I don't like your attitude."

Diego tried to keep me pinned, but I was taller than him by a foot. My biceps were almost as large as his head. Whispers were starting to spread through the cafeteria. *A fight!* Soon all noise had stopped. When he realized holding me was futile, he sprang back, his weapon in front of him.

"Your bitch turned one of my girls away," Diego said into the silence. "Says she's not putting out for my clients anymore."

I growled, my fists clenching. I should smash him for that. Screw my own rules about fighting in the cafeteria—it would be worth it to see his nose break. I kept my temper only with effort. Only because I hadn't yet found Bella.

"I don't know who you're calling a bitch," I said, through gritted teeth. "'Cause if you were to say that about Bella, I'd have to rip your balls off. So, I'm pretty sure we're not talking about her."

Diego spat. "If I find her, I'll cut her so bad that-"

The sentence finished in a squeak as my hand snapped out, grabbing him by the throat. My biceps flexed, and then I was slamming him into the wall.

"I lost a worker," Diego said, eyes bulging. His shiv clattered to the floor.

I didn't let go. "Explain."

"Ezzi came to me this morning saying she wasn't working for us anymore..." his face went red.

I growled, but relaxed my grip. "So?"

"She said she was under your protection." His eyes flicked past me to the crowd, and he raised his voice. "That's two girls you've stolen from me now. The Razors ain't gonna stand for that. You owe me."

Oh Bella, what have you done? I let Diego go, holding his gaze as I stepped back. He rocked on his feet and regained his composure.

I took a moment to consider my response. This wasn't about Ezzi. This was about saving face—Diego couldn't let his gang look weak. "Last I checked," I said, raising my voice to carry to the crowd, "Ezzi was a free agent. You employ her with your cocaína and your protection. If she doesn't want those, she has a right to leave."

Diego was rubbing at his throat. "Maybe if your bitch hadn't-"

I growled, cutting him off. "Watch your tongue," I said, fingers flexing. His words had ignited a protective anger in my stomach. I fought to keep my hands at my side. "You don't talk about her like that. Not if you want to live."

He spat. "I don't give a fuck what you say. You stole her!"

I leaned in close, my voice low enough that our audience couldn't hear. "I'm giving you a way out, you fool," I said. "This doesn't have to be a gang war. If you say she left on her own terms, we don't have to fight." I grimaced, not liking the words, but liking the alternative less. "Say she was useless. Say you kicked her out. Say whatever you want, and I'll support you. But if you ever, ever threaten her or Bella again..." I growled.

Diego's eyes went wide as he saw my fists clench. "You don't understand," he whispered. He looked as if he was about to cry. "I'm in a bind—I need Ezzi. I've got more clients than I can deal with, and if I don't provide, He gets angry."

He? Who was Diego talking about? Diego was the leader of the Razors. Did he mean the Warden? "Maybe you should take better care of your merchandise then," I said, shaking off the feeling that something wasn't right. I kept my voice low—two leaders having an angry conversation that the prison didn't need to hear. "If you didn't let your clients beat them, they might be happy to work for you."

"I can't help it. That's what he wants."

"The Warden?"

He shook his head.

"Then tell me who he is," I growled. "I'll make him change his mind."

Diego chuckled, finally getting his confidence back. His voice rose slightly. "You think you're all that, el Lobo. But he's untouchable."

A rumble sounded deep in my throat. "No one's untouchable."

"He's from the outside."

The rumble cut off. I stepped back. If this man that Diego reported to wasn't a prisoner, that was bad. Very bad.

Diego grinned triumphantly. "That's right, amigo. I might be fucked, but you are too. And when I find your bitch—the one who has caused us all these problems—I'm going to cut her so bad that-"

I roared, my fist was at his throat before I could help it, the Red flooding my vision like a wave. Air left Diego's body in a rush as I slammed him against the wall. *No one said that about Bella.* "I warned you," I said, struggling to form words when all I wanted to do was snarl. "I'll kill you right here, and go seven days without food, and it will be a pleasure."

He tried to speak, but my fist was too tight around his throat. I squeezed harder, enjoying watching his eyes bulge. It would be so easy to snap his neck for what he'd said about Bella. I lifted him slowly until his feet dangled. It would be so easy to throw him, or kick him, or snap him, or...

Something pierced the fog of fury in my mind. An image of Bella, holding me tight. Telling me in another confrontation with Diego, this one in the courtyard, that sometimes, anger wasn't the only way. He hadn't actually hurt her, and killing Diego would start a gang war. The prison couldn't afford that—it would just give the Warden more bodies to harvest.

I struggled against the urge. To pull the Red back, so I could see. "Touch her and I kill you," I said, lowering him back to the floor.

When I let him go, he sucked in a desperate lungful of air, scrabbling away. "You'll pay for that," he said.

"Just try it. You're the one that started the fight, remember?" I stepped toward him, and he cowered again. "But I'm the one that will finish it."

He ran toward the door, pausing in the doorway to glare at me. "You'll pay for this!" he called again. Then he disappeared.

Noise returned to the lunch room with a rush, but I ignored it, rubbing my fists as I stared after him.

This was bad. Very bad. Diego had a grudge to settle, but he didn't have Bella.

I had to find her before he did. I was starting to get worried. Where in el Castillo could she be?

22: BELLA

Darkness blinked away into a single bright light. Above me was a freshly painted ceiling. Beneath me was something soft.

It took me a moment to realize why that felt strange — Rio's bed was hard, like lying on a board, the mattress so thin it hardly counted. If my bed was soft, that meant-

I sat up suddenly, fighting the urge to be sick as the room spun. I was lying on a couch, and I wasn't in the prison — or at least, not a part of the prison I was familiar with. Beneath the scent of disinfectant that permeated the room I could still smell sweat and neglect, and maybe the faintest stench of weed. But the walls here were freshly painted, and the couch was plush leather, and beyond it was a coffee table full of magazines, then a computer on a big, fat desk. *Where was I?* A doctor's office?

A shadow moved in the doorway. "Ah, awake at last. The sleeping beauty."

I recognized that voice! I stood and spun, the movement blurring my vision again, and I reached out to balance myself on the coffee table. When my vision cleared, a familiar figure was standing before me.

"Gateau?" I asked, wondering just how badly I'd hit my head. My fingers reached up to probe the back of my skull, where they discovered a large, painful knot.

What the hell was he doing here? My brain spun, trying to make sense of what I saw, but it was like my thoughts were tires that had been stuck in mud. No matter how much I tried, they just kept spinning around and around, ending up back at the same place. I was in prison, but I couldn't be. Gateau was here, but he couldn't be.

"Bella!" Gateau said. It seemed he wasn't confused at all. "You don't know how good it is to see you safe after your time with those animals!"

"What… what happened to me?"

"Why, I'm here to rescue you, of course. These good for nothings you're socializing with are below people like us. It's time you stopped this foolish nonsense and came home." He smiled, but there was no warmth behind it.

"I… I don't understand."

He drew himself to his fullest height, the lines of his body hard and stiff. "Bella, it's time to leave the prison."

My brain was foggy, but I knew one thing for certain. "I can't, Gateau."

He moved toward me. "Not this silly nonsense about living conditions again? You're a white girl Bella. It's degrading to see you here with lesser people."

I pulled away from the racist creep, trying another tact. "Did you know, that they keep women here drugged against their will, so they'll be more willing prostitutes?"

"I'm sure that's not the case," he said, waving his hand dismissively. Something gold glinted on his wrist. A watch.

"It is," I said. "I spoke to one of the women myself."

"Women's gossip," he said. "You know what they're like."

I most certainly did. I was one of them. But I let the insult slide. "As soon as I get out, I'm going straight to the authorities. We'll get her to testify, and then-"

"Who is this woman?" he asked sharply. He paused, as if regretting his outburst. He dropped back suddenly, pulling himself together and flashing a grin that reminded me of the dinner we had shared. His fingers drummed on the desk with practiced familiarity. "That is to say, who makes this claim?" It was easy, even friendly, and a far cry from the scowl it replaced. But also, somehow... dangerous. The smile of a shark. "I'd like to question them personally, as this is such a serious issue."

"It's..." I paused, unnerved by that smile. He'd just been so dismissive of these people. Why was he now so eager to investigate? "Just a woman," I said. "One of many."

"What's her name?" he asked. "So I can protect her, of course."

"You have influence in this prison?"

He paused, his fingers leaving the desk. He fiddled with the watch on his wrist. "Of course not. What gave you that idea?"

"Then why would you want to know her name?"

He struggled with his answer, before eventually turning to face the wall, hands clasped behind his back. "Perhaps you are right, Bella. Maybe there is no need for you to go home just now. The women in this place need you."

I shook my head. I'd just said I wanted to stay, but at Gateau's words I suddenly wanted to leave. I'd been inside. I'd changed nothing. But outside—knowing about the organ harvests, and the prostitution—now I could make a difference.

Gateau didn't see the motion. He was still staring at the wall. "We'll keep you here, for the time being. Until I can get a grip on this organ business, and the prostitution ring that you're talking about."

I hadn't said anything about there being a ring. But that was beside the point, because it was true. "I'd like to go home, Gateau. I can come back, if I need to."

He shook his head, running a hand through his hair, that gold watch on his wrist tugging at a memory for an instant, before it was gone. "I wish it were that easy, Bella. You told the guards you were an inmate. I'll need time to organize the paperwork that proves otherwise."

"But... but..." Hadn't he just been talking about getting me out immediately?

He spun away from the desk and strode toward the exit before I could process what was happening. "Farewell, Bella. Be careful in here. I wish I could be more help."

"Gateau!" I cried, suddenly worried that he would leave. "Please, you have to get me out!"

He paused at the door. "I wish it were that easy, *chica*. Rest assured that I'm doing everything in my power to make this right."

The door closed.

The silence was deafening. *Why had Gateau changed his approach so suddenly?* One minute he had been hell-bent on getting me out, and the next he was telling me I had to stay in the prison. Was I truly an inmate here, now? I went to the door and tried to open it, only to discover that it was locked.

23: RIO

The gym had closed and evening set when I heard the patter of her feet—that light clip of her shoes which I hadn't known I'd recognize until they sounded.

"Bella!"

The footsteps faltered, then ran toward me even as I moved to the broken door leading into the hallway. The most beautiful vision appeared—a familiar face with dark hair, and a white dress.

"Ay, Bella, where have you been?" I said, catching her in my arms as she leapt toward me. I swung her around and into me with a choked sob. I'd been through all the public spaces in the prison once already, and had now been in the process of searching each again.

It took her several moments before she could talk. I held her as she caught her breath, catching my own in turn. Her soft body. The scent of her hair. I'd never admit it, but I'd been worried. Only now that she was back could I acknowledge the fears that had been running through my head.

"Rio, I had a run in with Gateau," she said as soon as she was able.

I eased her down, pulling her to sit at a weight bench constructed of an old board stacked atop bricks. "The man you told me about, with your father?"

She nodded. "When the guards came to get me, they said I was in the Apex."

A chill settled over me. I stood more quickly than I'd intended. "Bella, are you hurt? Did Diego…"

She shook her head. "Diego wasn't there. Just Gateau."

I crossed myself, glancing up to the heavens. "Thank the gods." Then I frowned, looking at her sharply as she sat below me. "What were you doing in the Apex?"

"I…" She frowned, her hand going to the back of her head, probing at something beneath her hair. She winced. "I blacked out. I think someone hit me. And when I woke up, I was lying on a couch."

"Did anyone…" I sat beside her quickly. Her dress was crumpled, but not ripped. If someone had hurt her, would it show?

She shook her head and I almost cried in relief, pulling her close. I said another quick prayer.

Then I pulled back, holding her at arm's length. "What did Gateau want?" I asked. I didn't like the guy. Had never met him, but still… I'd been around enough snakes in my time to know which creature he'd be if he was tattooed on my arm.

She frowned. "Well, first he told me he was sending me back home. But, then I told him about the prostitutes, and-"

"Wait," I interrupted. Maybe this had something to do with Ezzi. "What did you say about the prostitutes?"

She waved at me impatiently. "I'll get to that. I think there may be a way out of here—did you know that the Razors are bringing outside clients into the prison?"

I grimaced. I did. It was a dirty practice, but just another in a long list of things I was powerless to stop.

Beside me, Bella bit her lip. "So I said that to him, and then, suddenly, he changed his mind and said he couldn't get me out of prison, and left."

I sat still, processing the information. But Bella stood and began to pace. She moved to the concrete weights in the corner, running her fingers along them. Then the old rubber mat which I put down when people did stretches on the floor. "Here's the thing," she said, fiddling with a rolled up corner. "Up until then, it seemed like Gateau was going to pull me out." She turned to me. "Don't you think that's weird, Rio?"

I nodded.

"And the prostitutes—can you believe there's a secret entrance into this place? Ezzi said it was in the Apex. And I was just in the Apex! I know where it is!"

I hesitated. How did I tell her that I already knew all about it? And more importantly, why I knew?

"Rio?"

"I know about the Apex," I said quietly. I crossed to her, standing beside the mat.

She frowned. "How could you know about that?"

"I did favors for the Warden, before I met you. Things I'm not proud of. Some of them meant I needed to get outside the prison."

"The market," she said. Understanding slowly dawned across her face.

I nodded. "The Warden gave me small freedoms in return for buying what he couldn't be seen legally purchasing—bulk quantities of coca leaves, for example."

"We could get out of here!" she whispered, excited. She dropped the matting as sudden hope flared in her eyes. "It's just one door. We could break it down and-"

It broke my heart to cut her off, but the sooner she realized it was useless, the better. "It's impossible," I said, more harshly than I'd intended. "Don't you think every prostitute that's ever been through that door has thought

153

about it? Don't you think *I've* thought about it? *Secret* doesn't mean *unguarded*. There's more security on that side entrance than there is on the main gate." I ran a hand through my long, shaggy black hair—I'd have to bring scissors to it again soon. "Did you see guards while you were there?" I asked, my voice kinder.

She nodded. "Two of them dragged me out."

"And how many doors were you taken through?"

"Just the one."

"There's four more before you reach the outside. The brothel offices are first. That must have been where you were. But at the end of that corridor, there's a locked door into the brothel itself—a viewing parlor and then bedrooms off to each side. Get through the armed guards there, and there's another locked door. And then another. The last one is inch thick metal plate—most of the prostitutes don't know about that, they only go as far as the bedrooms. I'd have a better chance of ramming the front entrance down than fighting my way out of that final tunnel."

"But you *did* get outside."

I didn't answer. *How often had I wanted to run?* Once you were in that market, you were free. There were a million places to hide. But… the Warden had known that. That's why he'd picked me. Most people in this prison, they were hardened. But me, I had a weak spot. Always, when I left, the guards paid Ezzi a visit. They never finished their 'session' until I got back.

If one day, I happened to get lost in that market, and not return? Mateo would find himself without a mother.

"It's not an option," I said brusquely. I couldn't take everyone that I cared about with me. And that meant my only escape was in a body bag.

What was of more concern was Gateau. Something about him gave me the creeps. "Bella. A man like Gateau— he doesn't complain about what you're doing, *then let you keep on doing it*, unless he has something to gain."

I drew a deep breath, not wanting to say the words, but knowing that I must. "You need to leave. We'll get another message to your father. Tell him you're sorry. Tell him you want to go home."

She pressed up into me, biting her lower lip. "Could you leave like before—like when I saw you in the marketplace? We could get out of this country, go South. Just you, me... cocktails by the beach..."

I took Bella by the shoulders. 237. *No, now 238.* "I can't leave. But I need to see you safe."

"I won't leave without you, Rio."

"Don't you see!" My shout made Bella flinch. "I'm never leaving. I can't! But you... you have a chance at a better life."

My hands went to my face. I pressed the palms into my eyes, then dragged them over my ears to the back of my head. "I know what you're thinking," I said, quieter. "I don't *want* you to go." I looked at her, and my lips formed a wry smile. "I kinda like you, you know? But this isn't your world. I was so worried today! I could never forgive myself if you weren't safe."

She snuggled into me again. Her jasmine scent was so beautiful it made my eyes close. "You really like me?" she asked quietly.

I nodded, longing to say more, but holding my tongue. It wouldn't help if I said that now.

"I won't leave, you know," she said. *The stupid, stubborn, wonderful girl.* She looked up into my eyes, then stood on her tippy toes to kiss me in the middle of the gym. "Because I kinda like you too."

24: BELLA

He kinda liked me. That was more than I could ever have hoped. From someone like Rio, usually so stoic and silent, the words meant a lot.

I pressed closer to him, kissing him more firmly, wanting to take all the space between our bodies and replace it with us. He growled, and I melted. *Because I kinda liked him back.*

Then the kiss became firmer as he leaned over me, I was lifted in the air and my legs wrapped around his waist.

Soon we were up against a wall — rope hanging down on one side from some weird gym contraption, weights lying in neat rows at our feet. My arms ran around his neck, enjoying the press of his hot body into mine — the heat on my front a contrast with the cool of my back against the cold, hard wall. My toes curled in pleasure. I *loved* kissing Rio. There was something about his huge body that always quickened my breath. His hard jaw working against mine. His startlingly soft lips...

I sighed, enjoying the sensation. I could do this all day. Though actually… I kissed harder. Not all day. There were other things I wanted to do too.

"Let's go back to our room," I whispered between breaths. His head had dipped, nuzzling at my neck.

He shook his head. "We need to talk." But his kisses didn't stop, his lips travelling down my chest. "I don't like it when you leave."

"Really?" I broke out in shivers, my head leaning back.

He looked at me with a cheeky grin, and then lowered me onto my feet. "Yes." He spun me away from the wall, his hands pulling my top upward. "I'm going to teach you never to do it again."

He maneuvered me backward with a look in his eyes that made me go all gooey. I liked it when he was like this—all concerned and protective. My hands went involuntarily to my shirt, helping him raise it high.

He stalked forward again, pushing me back, ripping the top from my arms as soon as it had cleared my head. I bit my lip with a smile. *I liked it a lot.*

Now his hands went to his shirt, still stalking forward, still pushing me slowly backward. Glorious abs came slowly into focus, first as shadows, then in beautiful copper tones as his cotton shirt pulled up just like mine had. With arms crossed, he lifted it above his head, then threw it behind him.

The back of my legs bumped into something. I caught his hard waist to keep my balance. God, even my fingers touching him briefly made me hot. He didn't stop moving forward though. With a grin, he unwrapped my hands, then pushed me back. I overbalanced, falling to sit on the weight bench we'd talked on earlier.

The smooth, broad timber flexed slightly as my eyes became level with his crotch. *This was interesting.* I reached to caress the hard bulge of his pants. It seemed my kisses had had an effect.

He closed his eyes with a groan, but when I fumbled at his belt, they snapped back open. "Not yet," he growled. He pushed me again, this time so that I reclined back onto the bench. "I told you I didn't like it when you left." He got down on his knees, before me, and lifted my skirt up my thighs. "I'm going to teach you to never do it again."

Shivers ran over me as I realized his intentions. I couldn't help it; my legs parted involuntarily. "What if someone sees?"

He ripped off my panties. The moist cotton tore from my body like paper in his hands. "Let them watch."

"Rio, perhaps we should... Ooooooh."

His head buried between my legs and my thoughts turned to mush. With one arm behind me, the other grabbed at his shaggy locks of hair as his tongue parted my folds. "Rio..." I struggled to make sense, but again I couldn't get the words out.

When my third attempt was cut off in an inarticulate burble, I gave up, closing my eyes and throwing my head back. Who cared who saw, or who heard? I hoped someone did—I intended to make any hidden watchers jealous.

My mouth opened in a moan. Rio hadn't shaved today, and his rough whiskers tickled my thighs. They matched the movements of his tongue—up, down. In, out. I pulled at his hair. Dragged at his head. Thrills zipped through me, and I wanted him deeper inside.

"Rio, take your clothes off. Now."

He shook his head, the very movement sending ripples of delight through my body. Was this... allowed? To be the only one pleasured? To not have to do anything in return? I focused on the feeling between my legs—of his tongue has it brushed against my skin. The touch was so light and gentle it seemed inconceivable that it could be the thing pushing thunderbolts inside.

Was this allowed? I didn't know. And I didn't care. I was past doing anything but sinking back onto the bench as a Beast held my legs open and lapped pleasure into me.

Soon I was panting, the timber cool against my back, but my body startlingly hot. I reached up to rub at my bra, mirroring Rio's tongue in light flicks through the cotton on my nipples. Each motion, each movement, brought the promise of indescribable pleasure. When I lifted my head, I could see dark hair and a broad, copper brown back. The animals inscribed upon his left shoulder writhed and curled. The clock on his right arm seemed to move with the rolling of my eyes. It was getting harder to concentrate. I was seeing things. Soon, this pleasure would be too much.

"Rio. Soon." I couldn't gasp out more than that.

His efforts doubled, strong fingers spreading me like a petal, lapping at the sweet nectar inside. I wanted to howl like the wolf on his shoulder. Scream like the bat. My breathing quickened, breasts rising and falling as I fought back the pleasure that came next. "I can't hold on much longer."

My words only forced him deeper, till I couldn't tell where he started and I began. His tongue was a blur, and so was my heart. I crested higher, and higher, the peak just around the corner...

And suddenly he pulled back.

I gasped at the shock of the loss, blinking at him in dumb confusion. What had just happened. He was going to make me... make me... what was going on?

"That feeling right there? Of loss?" he said with a smug grin. "That's how I felt when I couldn't find you today."

"Rio..." Oh God. He was such a buzzkill! But also kinda... sweet. I tried to push his head back down.

He shook it, the shaggy locks flying from side to side. "Not until you promise not to run off again."

I was losing it. God, I was losing the orgasm. "Okay, okay. Whatever. I promise!" I tried to push him back down again.

Rio laughed, careless of the agony I was in. "I don't believe you."

A groan escaped my lips as he dipped down to lick just once, tenderly, between my legs. Sensation flared; a starburst in the night, and I cried out. *Nope. I hadn't lost it at all.*

Poised above my legs, Rio stayed silent, waiting for my answer. I gazed deep into his eyes as my body hummed, poised, and in that moment, *I knew.* When he'd said he 'kinda liked me,' those words had meant a lot. Rio was the Beast of the prison. With his tattoos and violent reputation, the only emotion he was expected to show was anger. Anything else was a… a weakness.

I bit my lip, finally understanding his request. "I promise."

His head dove back down at my answer, and pleasure spread back instantly through my body. It had never gone, just been poised, waiting for the words that would release it. I cried out as his tongue lapped at me, soon right where we had left off.

Oh God. He was so good! The laps were gentle, and then rough. Distant, and then pressing right down upon me. I began to gasp, breathing into an orgasm which was just around the corner.

His weakness. I was his weakness. This man who could fight off entire gangs. Who ruled more than a quarter of the prison. Who covered himself in the tattoos of his enemies, who even the guards treated with fear, was scared of losing *me*. The thought sent a thrill screaming through my body, bringing me closer to the edge.

I cried out as his fingers joined the fray—circling me as his tongue flicked just above, then when they were wet, diving deep inside. My eyelids fluttered. I fought the urge to let them roll back.

They pumped once. Twice. And then my back arched as they took me screaming over the edge. I cried out, my voice echoing up the concrete walls of the gym into the night sky. Rio's fingers stopped, curling inside me to hit my g-spot, and I screamed again, the sensation of his moving tongue and still fingers sending my voice skyward. When his fingers began to move, intent on bringing me to the edge again, my hands shot down to seize his head.

"What are you trying to do, make me fall off the bench? Come here." I pulled him up onto me. "I want you. *You*. Inside me."

He raised an eyebrow.

"Less sass, more undressing," I snapped. "It's the only way I can guarantee that you won't stop again."

25: RIO

Crude cries and the crash of an already broken door slamming against its hinges jerked me from blissful sleep. Dark shapes filled the doorway to the gym as I opened my eyes. I leapt to my feet. I knew immediately that we were in trouble.

"Bella, get behind me!" After our lovemaking session, we'd fallen asleep coiled in each other's bodies on the old gym matt. The night had been cool, but the heat of our bodies had lulled us easily to slumber.

We'd fallen asleep out in the open.

I was such a fool. Why hadn't we gone back to our room?

Bella jerked awake with a start. She cowered back, clutching at her clothes. "Get dressed," I commanded. I wasn't worried about myself. I crouched, naked, waiting for the shadows to resolve themselves.

"It's never enough, is it Diego?" I didn't need to see my attackers to guess who had paid us a visit.

Diego stepped into the room. "For once, I agree. Higher orders, I'm afraid." He eyed my cock, blinking in disbelief. "Fuck. Now I know why they call you The Beast."

"Get out of here. Last chance."

He laughed, motioning to people behind him. "Not this time." Five, ten, fifteen Razors crowded into the room. More kept coming. Too many to beat.

I could leap onto the chin up bar. Pull myself up and over the roof… I glanced at Bella, quickly getting dressed. *No. I wouldn't leave her. I would make my stand right here.*

I snarled. "It's me that you want. Leave her."

Diego laughed. "Oh, but that's where you're wrong." He pointed toward Bella. "Get her."

I leapt at the first gangbanger that approached, smashing my fist into him so hard he slammed unconscious against the wall. But the second was right behind him, and the third. One swung a baseball bat. I raised my forearm, blocking it. "Bella!"

A forth came in from the other side, swinging a metal post. I ignored it, too, batting the heavy beam away like it was made of foam. "Get into the corner. There's a metal bar near the weight bench. Use it!" It wouldn't be much, but we had to try.

More rushed past me, overwhelming my fists, which could only hit so many at once. Bella screamed as two Razors seized her. I spun to see her being dragged by the hair toward the door, and her name ripped from my throat.

The Red. The Red would come to my aid. The Red, my faithful companion. The Red, the only thing that could save us now. I roared, muscles bunching, as rage gave me strength. I threw my attackers off, shaking them like a bear, then leapt to save Bella just as she reached Diego.

Metal flashed. A sharpened spoon appeared at her throat.

I froze.

"Down, boy," Diego snarled. The bastard. He could've used it on me, but he'd known it wouldn't stop me, not when the rage overtook. What they'd needed, what the Razors had been lacking all these years, was a weakness that could drive me to my knees.

Diego's blade drew blood—a single bead, like the prick from a rose. It rolled down Bella's beautiful smooth skin. A sob escaped my throat. "Bella…"

"If you fight back, she dies. If you don't, I promise my men won't touch her."

The clubs didn't stop, but now, with the Red at bay, I could feel them. Slowly, I sank to my knees. The dull sound of them hitting my body filled my ears; made my head ring.

"Bella…"

She looked at me, terrified, and all I could do was sink to my hands now, like a dog, as the blows continued to rain down. I could hear the scuff of their shoes. The sound of their laughter. The beating of my heart. Bella.

They wouldn't hurt her, if I didn't fight back.

26: BELLA

I blinked against the light and shook my head, trying to rid myself of the fog that had settled over me. My eyes were heavy. I was thirsty, and had a metallic taste in my mouth. The scent of cheap air freshener, overpowering after my time in prison, made me want to wretch.

"Rio," I croaked. I had been with him but... my mind remained shrouded in fog.

The walls were clean and freshly painted, like the room with the couch where I'd met Gateau. And there was a couch in this room too, which I was laying on, but that was where the similarities stopped. I swung my bare feet down, confused. Cheap leopard print carpet lay underfoot. It was threadbare and had cigarette holes, but was luxurious after weeks spent walking on dirt. I looked around me in the low light at women who all looked like Ezzi with their long, dyed hair, and winged eyeliner. Many of them were in various states of undress.

"*Hola, Mami,*" said one girl with teased dark hair and blue eyes. "It's about time you woke up, eh? You were going to miss all the fun. Now the night is here, that's when the men start coming."

"The men?" I asked blankly. A piece of gum snapped in her mouth as she chewed it. Cheap silver bangles chimed on one wrist.

The girl laughed. "Of course. They like to come in the night. For a little relaxation, you know?" She gave me a wink, like we were in on the same secret.

I looked more closely at her—at the long expanse of exposed legs and short skirt, the tight top and overdrawn lips. The little room we all sat in had real furniture, even a grandfather clock in one corner. Multiple doorways led from the room, each bordered in long velvet drapes.

Like a parlor. A receiving room.

"I will tell the Madame that you're awake." The girl flashed me another smile—like I was a guest here and not brought against my will—before walking toward two men that I had previously not seen. They each had shaved heads, and wore dirty football jackets. *Razors*. She nodded to them, and they stepped aside. She ducked quickly through. Was I back at the Apex? I recalled Rio's description: past the offices was a viewing parlor, with bedrooms to either side.

"Welcome, welcome!" A woman arrived through the same door. She looked older and meaner than the girl who had left, and wore a long dark skirt and conservative blouse. Her hair had been swept up and back into a subdued up-do, to complement the subtle makeup on her face.

If she wasn't a prostitute, that could only mean she was…

"We hope you'll enjoy your little stay with us. I'm sure you'll fit right in here with my girls."

"Where am I?" I asked sharply. I was now very much awake.

"The Salon, of course," the woman said with a flick of her fingers through the air. "The heart of the Apex!" She gestured behind her. "I brought a friend to make your stay with us more comfortable."

Ezzi stumbled into the room, her eyes unfocused. "Bella?"

"Ezzi? Did they do something to you? Are you high?"

She burst into shrill laughter, and then sniffed, eyes going wide. "Of course. You will be too, when they give you your medicine." She giggled. "It makes all your problems go away."

"Where's Mateo, Ezzi?"

"Who?" she asked, distracted. My heart sank. Ezzi was on a cocktail of something—God knew what they had fed her, or injected her with.

"Ezzi, how did you get here? When?"

She smiled, laughing at a private joke. "Earlier, you know, after we talked, I stopped by the Razors and I told them, you know, maybe it wasn't for me." She sniffed. "I said I wanted to move upstairs. That maybe I could be something other than a Razor girl." Sadness seeped into her words. I saw it reflected in her eyes. "I went to your room to look for you, but you weren't there. The Razors were, though. They gave me something to drink. I don't know what happened after that."

Her voice became soft and detached. "It's not too bad. I've been here before. If you don't fight, it's not too bad." She brightened, though her eyes were still glazed. "Now you're here, too, maybe we can be a family! Just like if we'd stayed with el Lobo."

She reached over to pat me on the knee. I swallowed the panic rising in my throat. This wasn't where I wanted to be. I needed to get out of here. I needed to know if Rio was okay.

I needed to get away before they forced me to take whatever they'd given Ezzi.

A door swung open at the other end of the room and a man stepped in. As it was locked behind him, the Madame rushed over to take him by the hand. "Welcome, welcome," she said, just as she had to me, oozing solicitousness. "What can I get you today?"

He flicked his eyes toward her, then over the women in the room. His shirt was pressed and his pants were a crisp linen, his hair recently cut. This wasn't a prisoner, or a prison guard. This man looked and smelled expensive. *The stories about a side gate had been right.*

The girl I'd first spoken to—the one with the endless legs and snapping gum—tipped forward like she was getting a better view. Or maybe, giving a better view.

The man let his eyes linger on the shape of her before nodding back to the Madame. "That one there, then."

She squealed with delight and scurried toward him, wrapping an arm around his waist and draping herself over him. "Come on, *Papi*. Let's get you into something more comfortable."

She tossed another wink over her shoulder at Ezzi and me before leading him through a velvet curtain and then a door. Before she shut it, I glimpsed mirrors, and a four-poster bed.

The Madame drifted back toward us. "Look lively, girls. You must be like Marisol if you want to capture the attention of the men who come in. They don't come here for a wallflower they can pick up anywhere." Her hands spread. Her fingers wiggled. "They want something that *sparkles*."

Nothing like an abduction to diminish your sparkle. But it wouldn't be prudent to tell her that. "I don't belong here," I said instead. "And neither does Ezzi. There must have been some sort of mistake."

She smiled, hands closing. The sparkle also left her eyes. "Oh, but I think you do. I've seen you around prison, all prim and proper. Little white *gringa* thinking you're too good for us. Well, we'll see about that. The Razors have given you to me as a gift. They said you were curious about prostitution in the prison. That you wanted a firsthand experience."

My hands went to my breast. "I'm under Rio's protection. If you or any man here so much as touches me-"

She burst into laughter. "You must mean el Lobo? He can't help you here. This is Razor territory. Given to them by the boss man himself."

I bristled. "I'm no man's gift to give."

"They thought so too," the Madame said, gesturing to the girls. "They all find reason, though. You can find it in yourself to see your higher purpose here... or we can help you."

I looked around. Would Ezzi and the other girls help me if I made a move? Some of them, like that *Marisol*, looked like they enjoyed it here. There were many that didn't—I could tell because they were curled in balls on the couch, or stood with arms wrapped around themselves in corners. But most were like Ezzi—so drugged up they could barely see.

"I'm leaving," I said. If I had to, I'd do this on my own. "Try to stop me, and I'll claw out your eyes."

I pushed into the Madame, hand raised. Just as I'd hoped, she flinched, and in the confusion, I darted around her toward the door...

...to quickly find arms wrapped around my waist and neck.

"Hold her down," the Madame said behind me.

The Razors dragged me to the ground, one holding his dirty hand over my mouth and nose. Grime smeared like filth on my tongue when I opened my mouth to scream. I gagged, no sound coming out.

"We have ways of making you more cooperative, dear," the Madame said, standing over me. "Just ask your friend."

Bodies moved, then shortly my legs were pulled taught to the floor. No one came to help. Ezzi stood to one side, singing softly as she looked up at the roof. There were tears on her cheeks. She was singing a lullaby.

A hot pinch of pain in my thigh. I struggled, but my movements quickly became softer. Less forceful. Fire and ice was sliding through my veins. Then suddenly the men weren't holding me down. *I was floating.* A Razor stood over me, smiling a horrible grin, a needle in his hand. *Oh God. What did they give me?*

"I think this one needs a fuller understanding of her place," the Madame said, from somewhere far away.

The Razor with the needle laughed, and threw it to the floor. My vision swam, and a moment later the disgusting goon was inches away from me, his body pressed against my own. "Don't worry," he said. His smile showed yellow teeth. "I'll make sure you enjoy it."

Enjoy? What did he mean by that. Why was he so close to me? Why did the world ebb in and out, like my eyes were filled with water?

His breath smelled like his teeth looked — decay washed over me like a plague. One of his eyes was cloudy, I noted. There were pimples on his hairline, where he'd recently shaved.

"No." I heard someone speaking, but couldn't make out who it was.

… Why was I here? I waved the thought away. I had no time for it now. This man was going to do something nasty to me. Though… I suddenly couldn't remember what.

"No." That voice again. It seemed familiar.

The man smiled, and now I could see his breath in pretty colors and stars which swam around my head. He said something, though I didn't know what. It wasn't him that had been talking. Who, then?

Maybe I should ask the animals. They leapt around the room — pretty bunnies, and dirty hyenas. The grandfather clock was tap dancing. Butterflies fluttered over Ezzi's head.

Why were there animals in the room? Why was the clock singing *Be Our Guest?* If I could just stop spinning, maybe this kind man would let me up to ask.

"Stop fighting." I could hear him now. He was struggling, and I could feel my hands pawing at him, but why? He was on his feet, pulling me up. I must weigh a thousand pounds.

"No." The voice again, softer, but firm. My voice.

Oh God. The clock's song faltered. The butterflies disappeared.

For a moment, just one moment, adrenaline pushed the drugged haze back. *He was going to rape me*. He'd lifted me over his shoulder, motioned to a friend, and was carrying me toward a room.

In that moment of clarity, the full weight of what was about to happen hit me. They were going to lock the door, then lay me on the bed. They were going to...

My body responded to the horror in the only way it knew how. I reached deep within myself, and screamed so loud that even the hyenas covered their ears.

27: RIO

They beat me to the very edge of consciousness, and just when I thought they were going to give me one last kick and disappear back into the crevices they'd crawled from, they reached down and hauled me up, dragging me through the hallways.

My muscles made me heavy, but there were enough of them that they didn't struggle with my dead weight. I drifted in and out of the present moment as they paraded me through the hallways.

The smell of liquor and weed wafted at first like a vague memory, but grew heady in the air as we approached our destination. The feel of stale smoke weighed on me, smothered me. It reminded me of a life I had led before I ever made it into el Castillo. A time before prison. A time before Bella.

There'd been a different woman then. The only other one I'd ever... *kinda* liked.

I'd been different. Gentle. When she'd said I needed to prove my love, I got my first tattoo—her name, in small, elegant script upon my chest. When she'd said she needed more, she'd dragged my heart like my body was being dragged now—smearing it along the floor until it was so beaten that I would do anything—*anything*—to stop the pain.

The Razors dropped me with a thump. We had reached out destination.

I gently moved my arms and legs, feeling for stabs of pain or tightness, the telltale signs of serious damage. My shoulder clicked uncomfortably. I groaned, rolling onto my back and it clicked back into place.

The room was dark, though at first I couldn't be sure if that was a fact, or just seen through swollen eyes. Then a man stepped out of the shadows.

"I get to meet you at last, *el Lobo.* I've heard so much about you."

He hunkered down next to me, jabbing me in the shoulder emphatically. Stabs of pain shot up my arm. My shoulder wasn't completely fixed, then. "You who've been causing all this trouble. You who've been influencing the wrong people." He spat the words, full of contempt. "You used to be useful."

He pulled back abruptly, towering over me, only his polished leather shoes visible through my swollen eye. But I didn't need to see him to know I'd just been told I'd outlived my purpose in the prison. I wasn't going to live long enough to be troublesome to him again.

Which also meant I had nothing to lose.

I lay a moment longer, willing my body to respond. *But I was weak.* My body was weak. It had suffered too much. I was as shattered as the clock on my shoulder. The animals that decorated my body were all limping, licking their wounds, their tails between their legs. Bella had healed my heart, but she couldn't fix this.

Bella.

My mind flickered back to her first day in prison. I'd cared for 237 people then. Now I cared for 238. What would happen to her?

I knew the answer, and it made me want to growl. In a prison like this, the Razors would take her, and drug her, then rape her till she was broken—I knew it. I held my snarl back, not wanting my captor to hear, and found my hand clenching in anger.

Bella. The woman who had brought such joy to the children of the prison. My other fist flexed, joining the first as sparks of *Red* flickered in my heart. The fire had been doused, but it hadn't been extinguished, and as I remembered kneeling helpless before her, unable to fight back, her screams fanned that fire back into life.

I'd thought I was beaten, but it seemed my body knew better. Because as I thought about her—what she meant to me, what she had done for me—my pain began to fade, pushed back by a growing Red mist.

El Castillo had given me my rage, and Bella had taught me how to tame it. Now, somewhere in the middle, I discovered something else—that it could be *channeled*. That when the right cause came along, I could harness the energy that it gave me, and use it to perform extraordinary things. I could fuel it by thinking about her, and grow angrier and angrier, like a train building up steam. It fed my muscles and healed my pain through force of fury alone; a pressure cooker ready to burst.

I thought about Bella, and what would soon be in store for her. I thought about Bella, and the man before me didn't stand a chance. *The Red* exploded through my body.

I didn't stand. I *flew*, like an angel on wings of vengeance, my fist colliding with my captor's stomach so hard that his feet lifted off the ground.

He crashed to the leopard print carpet, his head bouncing off the floor with a satisfying crack. I turned, snarling, to face the other men in the room. As one, they stepped back in horror at the beast that stood before them.

I leapt forward; a wolf that had slipped its leash.

They weren't fast enough to escape, and I dove into them, enjoying the satisfying snap of a shoulder under my hands, a Razor crying out in pain, before my arm snaked around another's neck, hauling him against me. As he turned blue and slid to the floor more appeared. I didn't give them time to react. Muscles flexing, I plowed into them, smashing fists against collarbone, jaw and navel. When someone grabbed my arms from behind, to slow me down, I slammed my head back, breaking his nose. I was el Lobo. The Beast. And I would kick and bite and break anyone who got between myself and my woman.

The last Razor slid to the floor from a headbutt. I stood panting above him, the room full of blood and bodies, and only then realized that I was still naked. I stripped a nearby razor of his pants. He woke briefly, looking toward the man with the polished boots and attempted to say a single word. "Ni-"

He slumped again, unconscious.

My head snapped to follow his line of sight. Who was this man in the black leather shoes? Someone important, I had no doubt. A gold watch flashed on his arm, and I frowned as a memory tugged at me. I recognized it, but from where?

In the distance, Bella screamed.

My body stiffened. That scream hadn't been in my head. Bella was in trouble. Instantly, *the Red* was back, a switch that had been tripped by a fair maiden's hand. The mystery of the watch, I could worry about later. Bella needed me now.

I raced toward the door, hoping I'd be able to pull it open—it was locked, but gave so easily it should be paper. I smashed through it into a sterile corridor I didn't recognize. To my right I could see the end of the hall; to the left, in the distance, a room with velvet drapes. I loped toward it through the dim hallway.

Two Razors stood guard at the entrance to the brothel. They never stood a chance. When they slid down the wall and hit the floor, I took the key from one of their belts and opened the door.

Several girls screamed when they saw me. I knew why—in their eyes, a huge man, seven-foot-tall and covered in blood and tattoos had just invaded—but I didn't care. They weren't the woman I was looking for.

I scanned the room in frustration. My eyes alighted upon Ezzi. "Where is she?" I demanded, striding forward. Two Razors from the opposite doorway leapt toward me, but I was unstoppable. They crumpled, and I stepped over them, my eyes intent on my prize.

The poor woman didn't answer, she just stood, rocking back and forth. They'd done something to her. Something bad. She was humming a lullaby.

"Ezzi!"

"Family," she croaked. "She's family, now."

I growled in frustration. But then a cry sounded from one of the adjoining rooms. *Bella!*

I didn't stop to think. I launched myself toward the door, crashing into it. It splintered, then fell forward under my weight in a flap of velvet curtains. Beyond it, Bella was on the bed. Her dress was ripped. Two Razors stood over her. One was undoing his pants.

With a roar, I surged forward. Their hands rose in surprise, but they might as well have blocked a sledgehammer. Heads snapped back. They were both unconscious before I picked them up and threw them into the wall.

"Bella." I seized her shoulders. Her clothes were still on—that was a good sign. "Are you okay?"

She fought me briefly. She had a glazed look in her eyes.

"Bella. We need to get out of here."

Her reply was a burbling giggle. She spoke a series of words that only made sense in her mind.

I picked her up, feeling her small, frail form against my bare chest. Anger welled up within me, but I forced it down. I could control the Red now. It had served me well.

I stepped back into the main room, thinking quickly. Where could we go?

I had a key now, for the third locked door. I looked longingly at the entry I had come through. That meant I could make it almost to the outside. Freedom was so close it was only inches away.

But... those inches were solid metal, and the last door not so easy to break. Even if I could make it beyond it? Before we got outside, there would be armed guards. I couldn't risk Bella being shot.

We would have to go back inside the prison. But... not to my quarters. Somebody wanted Bella broken and me dead. Somebody from the outside, who had access to the Razors, and to the guards.

Where could we hide?

A memory came to me, of a little boy leading me by the hand, and a room full of boxes. There was one place we might hide until things cooled down. The place Mateo had shown me. The best spot for hide and seek. He'd been so proud to have something he could give to me, instead of the other way around.

It might just save us now.

Cradling Bella in one arm, I bent to pull the key to the second door—back into the prison—from an unconscious Razor. Then I strode to grab Ezzi by the wrist. "We have to be fast."

She nodded, seeming to understand. I unlocked the door, then turned to the other occupants of the brothel. "Those here by force, you are free to leave. Those here by choice, you are free to stay." Near half the women followed me out the door.

Lumen was waiting for me when I reached the outside.

"Ay, Rio, I didn't think I would see you again," he said, women streaming out behind me, running back into the prison. "What I heard, what I saw-"

"Forget it Lumen. I need you to be my eyes." The Red was still there, behind my vision, but it was controlled now—a tool that I would bring out when required. "I'm taking Bella someplace safe. I need you to get Ezzi back to Mateo. Look after her. Then get another message to her father and tell him he needs to act, *now*. When you hear back, tell Mateo to find me."

"How will he know where to look?"

"Tell him I'm playing hide and seek."

Lumen frowned, but took me at my word. "You got it, Rio. I'll let you know as soon as I find out."

28: BELLA

I didn't know why Rio had taken me here, only that I trusted him, and I was safe. The room was tiny. And dark. I could hear him panting beside me. When I touched his body, it was slick with sweat.

"Rio? What's happening?" There'd been dancing animals, and a clock singing a song, but they were gone now, disappeared into the darkness.

He shifted beside me. "We'll wait here for the night."

"It's nice," I said. And it was. The room felt like our own, private hideaway. If we ever needed to hide from people, this would be a great place to start.

A dizzying sensation passed through me, and I stumbled. Why did needing to hide worry me?

It all came flooding back.

I stumbled again, this time in fear. "Rio! He was going to…"

He held me tight. "I know. But you're safe now."

I slid down to the floor. Safe. In Rio's arms, I was safe. The thought instantly calmed me. As Rio dropped to sit at

179

my side, my heart stopped its furious beat. *Rio had saved me. Everything would be alright.*

"Do you promise, Rio?"

Beside me, I felt him shift in the darkness. "I'll do everything I can."

I shook my head. It wasn't enough. "You need to promise. Promise you'll always be there." It was hard to remember what had been real, and what had been the drugs. "Promise me that you'll always be there to fight the hyenas and the talking clocks."

"You're still high."

I rested my head against him, considering the question. "Just a little," I said, realizing it was true. "What did they do to me?"

He growled, a deep rumble that reverberated through his chest. "I don't know. But when I find out, I'll…"

He broke off as I stretched over and began to pat him on the head. "There, there, kitty. It's okay. You saved me."

A snort, as if in sudden laughter. "You're *so* high right now."

My eyelids fluttered as the silence began to weigh on them. The hand that had been patting Rio's head drifted down his face, tracing the scar on his chin, and then fell to his chest. In the dark, my fingers brushed against his scar. *The patch of skin he had scraped off with a knife.*

My head popped up, briefly. "Rio?"

"Yes?"

A finger traced the outline of the scar. "What was the tattoo of, Rio?"

He stiffened, but then relaxed. "A woman's name," he said. He sounded tired, just like me.

"Did you like her?"

His arm stretched behind me, pulling me into a hug. "You're high. Stop asking so many questions."

I giggled. Maybe I was a *little* high. "Just answer it."

Rio was silent, for a while. "She's the reason I'm here," he said eventually. "I thought I loved her. She didn't love me. That's all you need to know."

His hand rested on my head, brushing my hair softly. "No more questions now. It's time for sleep."

A shiver started at the base of my skull and tickled all the way down my back. I couldn't tell if it was the gentle strokes on my head, the drug wearing off, or Rio's presence beside me. I settled against him in the dark, snuggling into his side.

I was almost asleep when he shifted. "Bella?"

I blinked my eyes open, struggling to stay awake. "Yes?"

"I promise," he said gruffly. "I'll all always be there, to fight the hyenas and the talking clocks."

I smiled, in the dark, then allowed my eyes to close.

29: BELLA

I awoke to a stiff neck and distant, hazy memories of Rio fighting off crazed animals. The image made me frown until I sat up with a jerk.

The parlor! There had been a Razor standing over me, loosening his belt!

Beside me, Rio pulled me into a hug. "Shh. You're safe now, gata salvaje."

Rio. Rio had protected me. He'd burst into the room and fought off my captors. He'd carried me to safety. He'd sat beside me in the dark. "Thank you."

"How do you feel?"

I pondered the question. All things considered, I could be a hell of a lot worse. "I feel thirsty," I said. "And grateful."

Rio snorted.

I snuggled into his side. "Though not necessarily in that order."

He disentangled himself briefly to reach for something. It was a bottle of water. "Here."

He must have left, sometime while I was asleep. "How long was I out?" I asked, gulping the bottle down gratefully.

"About four hours."

The cool liquid slid down my throat so fast it was gone by the time he'd finished speaking. "That tastes so good I could kiss you!" I said, feeling instantly better.

I paused, considering the question. "In fact, I think I might." I rose slightly to kiss him on the cheek.

He laughed. "My pleasure."

I leaned back against his chest. With my head pressed against him, I could faintly hear his heartbeat, and the rhythm of his breath. "Did you sleep?"

He shook his head. "I made you a promise."

At his words, more memories came flashing back. Rio setting me down when we reached the hiding place. Me giggling in the dark. Me peppering him with questions. "Oh God," I said, scrabbling to my feet. "I'm so sorry about that. I had no right to ask you…" I grimaced, silently blessing the shadows which hid my bright red flush. "I was high, it's my only excuse."

He stood, a whisper of clothing beside me in the dark, then pulled me into a hug. "I meant it. I'll protect you, always."

Dim memories of Rio fighting off my captors flashed back to me. Blind, I ran my hands over him—finding the fists which had protected me. I explored them with my fingers. They were rough, at the knuckles, where they'd obviously been cut.

My fingers moved up his body then—over a firm stomach contoured with abs to his broad chest. It had bunched, I remembered now, and thrown two men across a room. His skin, so hot and slick when we'd entered here before I slept was now cool and dry to my touch.

We were alone, and I was safe, and on the wave of my relief a new sensation shivered across my skin.

This one was centered between my legs.

"You've done so much for me," I whispered. I pressed against him, but in a different way than before. This time, my hips moved against his thigh.

"It was nothing."

I shook my head. It wasn't nothing. *It was everything*. An urge was building within me—a raw, powerful need to show my gratitude with more than just grateful words. This man was my protector. He'd saved me.

I stood on my tip toes to kiss him. He'd fought for me. He'd won me.

"Take off your pants, Rio," I whispered.

"We can't. We're supposed to be hiding. We have to be quiet."

His hands rested on my shoulders, but I knew the truth. I could feel the bulge growing against my thigh. My hands snaked down his pants.

"Um…" he tried to move away from me, but the confines of the room were small. My hands remained where I had placed them. "Bella…"

He grew firmer within my grasp, and I giggled. "I know you want it. Just like I do. Doesn't Prince Charming always get a kiss after rescuing the princess in fairytales?"

"I'm no Prince Charming," he growled. "I don't think we could be quiet."

I dropped to my knees. "I don't think so either. That's why this is all about you—here, let me give you my kiss."

I worked my fingers over the clasps of his pants. He pushed at my hands gently, but I pushed back, and soon he was released. He sprung free—I could feel the whisper of air close to my face—and in the dark I guided the hard tip to my mouth, kissing it gently.

"Bella…"

He was trying vainly to resist me, but I knew I had him now. He'd pleasured me so wonderfully, in the gym. Now, in the dark, it was my turn to pleasure him in return. The only difference here was, he couldn't make a sound.

"Shush," I whispered. "Lean back. Relax." I lifted his bulk slightly, positioning myself beneath, then licked from the base to the tip.

He groaned. His hands clutched at my hair. I knew his will had broken.

In the dark, everything was different. I'd seen him before, of course. I'd marveled at his size and bulk. But now? With my sight gone, my other senses came alive. He was so hard he throbbed, but also soft—muscle wrapped in the silk of a market scarf. My lips slipped over his tip. My tongue lapped out. He tasted… good. His scent was that of musk and soap.

My mouth slid down him slowly, exploring him, enjoying his bulk against my tongue. Above me, he shivered. *My savior.* I pulled back up, then slid down again, lubricated, to show him my thanks. I wanted to do this for him. For me. They'd tried to take my body, but he had saved me. As thanks, he could have it whenever he might want.

His breathing was slow at first. Measured. I placed one hand on his hard stomach as I knelt before him, the other at his base. It moved in time upon him with my mouth. When I twisted my wrist, once on the way up, the other way as I went down, his breathing grew faster. I grinned, my lips tightening in pleasure around him.

"Bella." In the dark, there was only his voice, and his body. My legs clenched together, a tingle zipping through me. I hadn't touched myself... but I wanted to. There was something about my muscled protector, standing over me in the dark that was… hot.

A hand drifted between my legs, and found me all wet. *Very hot.*

One hand on him, the other on me, my lips left his tip and trailed down hard silk to the sack beneath. His tuft of hair, course and thick, tickled my nose as I took a different part of him in my mouth. I'd heard there was a different sensation here, for a man. Something that added richness to the feeling above. I sucked on them, like delicate cherries, then moved my lips slowly back up.

His hard surface was slippery now with my saliva. His tip, I discovered when my tongue flicked out, had beaded with his own display of pleasure. He was as wet and slick as I was between my own legs.

My head and hands moved together in time, the sound of my soft sucks a counterpoint to his hard breathing, and my own quickly escalating gasps. The ridge of his end tickled my tongue. I flicked over it—he moaned. *So he liked that*. I twirled my tongue around him. His noises, despite his attempts to be quiet, began to echo off the walls.

My savior. How many times had he protected me now? It seemed too many to count. I moved faster, tongue swirling, hands moving, driven by desire, and pleasure, and an overwhelming urge to thank him for what he'd done. *No*. More than that. To *show* him what he meant to me. To give him physical proof that I was his, and he was mine.

His hands settled in my hair, twisting through my locks. And then he was lifting me, pushing me against the wall in the dark. His strength frightened and delighted me. He lifted my dress urgently. I pushed my underwear aside.

I cried out as he entered. I couldn't help it—eventually bringing my hand up to cover my mouth. I'd thought my hands between my legs enough, but this... this was something else. That sweet and salty taste on my tongue was now between my legs. The pleasure I'd given him had been returned ten-fold.

I clutched at him as we began to move—no softness now, no foreplay—urgent motion escalating from a standing still start. He slammed into me, over and over. I threw back my head, clawing at him. We were two wild animals mating in the dark. "Rio.... I can't..." I was so close to orgasm I couldn't finish the sentence, just hold on and enjoy the ride.

Pleasure passed through me in waves, urging me to keep going, until finally he swelled inside, and we both gasped. My lips found his. My eyes rolled back. He slammed me up against the wall, then was still, his buttocks straining, biceps bulging, as inside, he moved of his own accord. The force of his pleasure sent my own shockwaves soaring. I tightened against him. My lips found his, muffling my cries. Though it was dark, so dark I couldn't see him, suddenly I saw the light.

When our shared trembling subsided, we collapsed against one another. I'd thought I'd been high this morning. It seemed in Rio, I'd stumbled into another.

30: RIO

It was easy to lose track of time in the room. We slept and touched and that was all there was to do. I slipped out, briefly, to find water. It was approaching evening, the shadows long, but I dared not linger.

When I returned, Bella gulped the liquid down like it was the most wonderful, beautiful thing anyone had ever done for her. "Ay…" She muttered, hand massaging her forehead. "Delayed hangover." But even through the pain, she managed to smile.

We were alive. And she was safe. Everything else was inconsequential.

We made love, to help her headache disappear, and then laughed at our poor excuse afterward. I'd dressed to slip out for more water when there was a loud noise at the storage room door.

"Quick." I shot her a look. She scrabbled for her dress, all thoughts of drinking forgotten.

I tensed as boxes scraped across the floor. But then a series of raps—some fast, some slow—sounded on the door.

That was Morse Code! One soft rap. One loud rap. Three soft raps. Three loud raps. *'Rio?'*

I tore the door open and scooped Mateo into a huge hug.

He laughed, squirming from my grip, then signed at me. I squinted at the gestures in the light from the open door.

"What's he saying?" asked Bella. "Is everything alright?"

I frowned, concentrating on his words. When he was finished, I asked him to repeat it. He did so, taking great care to ensure I understood.

Bella was waiting impatiently at my shoulder. "Well?"

I turned, heart hammering. "Your father has received the message we sent to him," I said, struggling to control my emotions. "He's begun the process for a review of the prison. You will be released."

Bella's hands clapped to her mouth.

I broke into stunned laughter. "Mateo says I'm to be moved as well."

"What?" she cried, rushing toward me. "That's amazing! And impossible."

I shook my head, so blindsided by the news that I wasn't quite sure how to react. "Apparently, it's been in process since you walked out on your father." I broke into an unsure grin. "My own extradition is more recent, I'm told. Another prison, but a better one, while my case is in review. We need to get back to my room and… and…"

I stopped speaking, the enormity of my news finally washing over me. "I'm leaving." I laughed, grabbing Bella by the hands. "Bella, I'm leaving this shithole."

She laughed along with me. We both did a little jig, which made Mateo laugh. "It couldn't happen to a nicer convict," she said.

I lifted her into the air and spun her. "Where will I go?" After here, another prison would be a paradise. Hot showers. No looking over my shoulder. *A chance at starting again.* I lowered her into a kiss. Mateo made a grossed-out noise behind us.

My forehead lowered to rest against hers, her face almost blurry in its closeness. "Come on, we should go."

"Is it safe?"

I nodded. "We should be careful of the gangs. They'll want vengeance. But if we can get to my room, I can lock the door. Only the guards have the key—" I grinned, "— and now, they're on our side."

We let Mateo leave first—gave him distance so nobody would suspect he'd been involved in helping us. I told him to go back to his mother, who he said had a headache but was otherwise doing okay. I advised him to get her water.

Bella squeezed my hand as I pulled her, looking left and right, into the hall.

When I'd first come here, I'd been convinced I'd never leave. The things I'd been party to—lord knows I didn't deserve freedom. I'd been a broken man then, with blood on my hands and a shattered heart.

I'd thought I was better, eventually. Pumping iron, lifting weights, growing strong. My body had healed, but my heart never had. I just hadn't realized it until Bella came along.

We breathed a sigh of relief when I turned and locked the door to my room. "Rio," Bella said, turning to face me. She grabbed me by a hand. "Thank you for everything." Her other hand rose to my face, cupping my cheek. Her fingers traced gently over my scar. "I can't tell you what this has meant to me. I can't imagine going back to a time when I didn't know you."

I drew a breath, to tell her she didn't need to say it. But she shushed me with a shake of her head. "I want you to know I'm not going to let things change when we leave here. I'm not going to walk away from you. I want this."

Her eyes glittered in the dark room, they caught the light of the just rising moon as it spilled in through the window, and she gave a short laugh. "I mean, not *this*," she said, gesturing to the prison at large. "I definitely don't want any more of that." A nervous giggle escaped her. "But you. Us. I can't imagine a life where we're not together."

My hands rose to meet her face, mimicking her fingers on mine. I leaned down, to kiss her on the mouth. "That suits me just fine, *gata salvaje.*"

We gazed into each other's eyes until the enormity of what was happening washed over me. "I'm leaving," I said, eyes blinking. "I'm actually leaving."

She laughed. "Well what are you waiting for? Start packing! I'm not hanging around when they arrive!"

I scanned the room. Most of what I had, I would leave here. But there were a few precious items I'd pack away — a polished stone that Mateo had given me when we first met. An old tattered book I'd read a hundred times. I pulled a small canvas bag from beneath my mattress and moved around the room, collecting the things that meant something to me, one by one.

"I'll need to tell the other leaders I'm leaving," I said, thinking through all the things I had to do before I went. "Should I dissolve the gym, or leave it to the community?"

Bella shrugged, enjoying the look of excitement on my face. This was really happening!

"Lumen can have my room. I'll have to tell him that he's in charge," I said, picking up an old t-shirt and throwing it into the bag. Lumen wouldn't want it, and you never knew...

Lumen.

I stopped suddenly. *Lumen. Ezzi. Mateo.* They weren't leaving.

Shame washed over me as my shoulders slumped. "How can I rejoice when so many will be left behind?"

Bella's eyes were soft. "You can't save them all, Rio."

"It's just not right."

She shook her head. "Trust my father, he'll fix this." She raised an eyebrow. "When I was little, he used to search my room. He's very thorough when he thinks someone is up to no good."

I nodded and she kissed me. But I went back to packing with a slightly heavier heart.

"You know," Bella said as she watched me. Her arms were folded as she leaned up against the wall. "Wherever you go, I imagine they'll allow visitors."

"We'll see," I grumbled.

"Relax," she said. She reached out as I passed her, running her fingers through my hair. "I got in here. I can get to you anywhere."

I chuckled at that, slightly happier.

"And I'll bring you presents! Tacos."

"Ay…" I said absently, still thinking about Lumen. But then I stopped, her words sinking in. Tacos. *With real meat.* "Could you do that?" I asked hesitantly, hardly daring to hope. "Bring them in?"

She laughed. "They'll probably serve it!"

I licked my lips. "What about Coca-Cola? I used to love Coca-Cola."

She grinned. "If they don't, I'll smuggle one in." Her arms spread wide. "I'll bring you a smorgasbord of contraband, wrapped up in a picnic basket."

We laughed together, and then a quiet settled over us.

"And maybe," she said, "you'll get out early."

She still didn't know. But it wasn't right to bring down the mood. I forced a smile. "I've never been accused of having good behavior before."

There was a knock at the door. A strident rap which spoke of authority. Bella looked to me, hope etched across her face.

"Who is it?" I called.

Sharp voices from outside; one, I recognized. I frowned. "That sounds like Diego."

A key scrabbled in the lock.

"Bella, get behind me." I pushed her back as the door burst open. A tall man with polished shoes, a gold watch and a black eye walked in carrying a gun. He was followed by Diego and twenty Razors.

31: BELLA

"Gateau?" I asked, stepping beside Rio. "What's going on?"

Rio growled when I mentioned the name. "I should have known." He started forward.

Gateau lifted his gun. "Keep your dog on a leash." He winced, as if moving suddenly had hurt him.

I staggered back. *Gateau was here to rescue me, wasn't he?* Where were the guards? And why were the Razors standing at his back?

"Gateau?" I asked. I felt like a broken record, just saying the same thing over and over. His smile didn't reach his eyes. Behind him, Diego sniggered. Little chunks of information started to fall like pebbles in the landslide of my mind.

Gateau had gone to the guards.

The Guards worked with the Razors.

The Razors hated Rio.

My hand went to my mouth with a gasp. What lies had they told him? That I was being held hostage? Worse? "You've got it wrong," I whispered.

Gateau shook his head. "I should have never let it get this far." He gestured at me. At my tattered prison dress and messed up hair. "Look at you! Dressing like a whore, associating with criminals like they're your equals."

My hands went to my mouth. Gateau sighed. "You have been causing me a lot of grief, Bella—here at the prison, and at work with your father. He actually thinks things need to change!"

"They do!"

Gateau shook his head. "These men are rapists and murders. They deserve everything they get. We can't change their history any more than they could suddenly become intelligent and white. We can only lock up those who refuse to conform."

I stared blankly at him for a moment. His argument was flawed on so many levels that I didn't know where to start! You couldn't change history, but you could atone for it, couldn't you? And what the hell did the color of someone's skin have to do with anything, let alone how smart you were?

Behind Gateau, Diego was frowning too.

I reached out for Rio's hand, my soft white skin gripping his tanned, calloused fingers firmly. "You're mistaken, Gateau. No one deserves a prison like this. Rio is being moved to another one, and after, I'm going to get this one closed down."

Gateau sighed. "You were so much better when you were just a picture on Facebook. It's time for the men to talk now." His eyes flicked to Rio, and hardened. "El Lobo. You're convicted of bribing an official, disrupting an authorized rehabilitation program, and attempted escape."

"What?" I started forward.

Rio held me back, like he already knew what was coming. "Bella," he said, defeat in his voice. "Don't."

"What do you mean don't? You've done nothing wrong!" I turned on Gateau. "You're full of shit."

Gateau smirked. "El lobo," he said, addressing Rio. "Were you, or were you not in the women's rehab center yesterday?"

Rio growled. "There was no *rehab* there, and you know it."

Gateau smirked. "I'll take that as an admission of guilt." He turned back to me. "And then there was his attempted escape. Did you know he made it all the way to the fourth door? It was only by the brave intervention of Diego and his team that we were able to stop his escape."

Diego was still frowning, behind Gateau, but at his words, his chest puffed up.

"My father will stop this," I said, fists clenching.

He laughed. "Isabella, you're lucky your father hasn't been indicted on criminal charges. It was only through my personal intervention that it didn't happen. There are multiple records of this... *Latino*... beside you conversing with him about escape."

I threw up my hands. "It was *my* escape! I shouldn't have been in here!"

Gateau blithely ignored me. "Do you know what the penalty is for trying to pervert justice?" He gestured around him. "How long do you think your father would last in here?"

"It's a mistake!" Surely Gateau could see that. Surely this was all just a big misunderstanding.

He shook his head. "Bella, this must all be so confusing, I know." A smile spread across his face like oil on water. His voice was patronizing. "You've been stuck here for *so* long, I honestly can't blame you for picking the wrong side. You're a victim here."

"Rio's innocent."

Gateau sighed, and tossed a folder, which he took from Diego, at my feet. "Before you decide, you might be interested in knowing exactly what put him here in the first place."

Photos spilled from the folder. Against my will, I leaned down to pick them up. In the pale moonlight streaming through the cell's window, I made out a scene of shattered plate glass, blood smeared floors... and bodies.

It was a photo of bloodied bodies in a bank. *A robbery gone wrong.*

The next photo was of a victim, eyes wide and staring. Her hair had been coifed, as if she were about to go out, but her face was bloody and white. Next came an old man. Then a younger one in a suit. I kept flicking, unable to stop myself. Men, women, young, old. Nobody had been spared. The last photo was of Rio and another woman, both wearing heavy handcuffs on their wrists.

Gateau laughed at my expression. "Twenty-three people dead, including one infant. Police at the time called it the most gruesome, wanton act of destruction they had ever seen."

"Rio?" I whispered, urging him to defend himself. *He was quiet.*

I wanted to be sick. It didn't seem possible. That the man I had come to know could have been involved in anything like that? I looked toward Rio, hoping he might be able to provide a rational explanation for what had happened. When he didn't meet my eyes, a terrible chill settled over me. Had everything I'd thought I'd known become a lie?

"You may come with me," Gateau said stiffly. He pulled something from his pocket as the Razors poured out from behind him to encircle Rio. "Your boyfriend... will not be so lucky."

Gateau let his eyes linger on me for a long moment. Then he spun on his heels, motioning me to follow.

He stopped only to drape a pair of rosary beads on the door.

32: RIO

The walls of this part of the prison corridors were obnoxiously small. When the Razors couldn't fit on either side, they boxed me in, shoving me from one to another. When no more than a single man could fit shoulder to shoulder, they pushed me from behind.

If I'd been half the man I was 20 minutes ago, I would have broken each of their faces in turn. Instead I just took each push in stride as my feet led me past the main entrance, away from freedom, and down a dark, cramped corridor.

My rage was an engine that wouldn't start, a fire that just would not catch. All the fuel was there, but something had smothered it, drenched the coals and sucked out all the air. I'd thought I could channel it. But I was wrong. I searched for it in my body, but I couldn't even find a spark.

I'd known what was coming, as soon as Gateau had entered the room. There'd been rage then, but as soon as Gateau raised his gun? All that rage had fled.

I had experience with guns, didn't I? I knew the damage that they could do, in another's hands. In a room as small as my cell, with Bella beside me, I couldn't risk one going off.

Bella. Why hadn't I been brave enough to tell Bella about Elizabeth? To explain why there was a scar on my chest where her name had once been. But it was too late now, wasn't it? Maybe they'd let me tattoo Bella's name on my body before I died.

When we reached my cell, a Razor sent me careening into the far wall with a final kick. Hoots of laughter drifted away from me behind the slam of the cell door.

I felt my way around in the dark. I knew where they would have taken me, but my insipid hope had deep roots as I marked out the perimeter of the room. It didn't take me long to finish—smooth walls on three sides, broken only by a thick pipe that ran from floor to ceiling, too well secured to move. Metal bars on the fourth—a cage, with the door securely locked. An isolation cell. Even my roots of hope withered and died.

I knew of the isolation cells, of course, but I hadn't spent any time in them. In a place like el Castillo they didn't care much what you did, as long as you weren't on death row.

But once you were? Isolation was your second to last stop.

Good. Life hurt too much to continue the fight.

It hurt too much to think about Bella—the look on her face when she realized it was Gateau who had come to rescue her. It hurt too much to remember the horror on her face when she realized what those photos were pictures of.

It was better that she didn't know the truth. She was gone now. Safe.

Still, it had hurt, watching her leave. Just like the last woman in my life, she wouldn't come back.

33: BELLA

In the dark of night, the market looked entirely different. No one was around, the stalls were empty. It was hard to imagine that every morning the locals had to set up their wares all over again—just to take them down when the day was over.

The guards walked with me to my front door—Gateau had escorted me from the prison, then said he had one last thing to do before he left, and would meet me later. It was surreal, opening the door and stepping through the threshold, like I had never missed a day. Like I hadn't spent the last few weeks living in a prison.

My father waited in the front room, sitting rod-straight in one of the caned chairs, a drink in his hand.

"Bella!" he cried, jumping to his feet and rushing toward me, wrapping his arms around me in a hug so tight I could barely breathe. "*My flower!* I am so happy to have you home again."

It felt so good to fall into his embrace. I took a deep breath and inhaled his scent. Though I laughed in happiness to see him, tears stuck at my eyes, threatening to slide down my cheeks.

How bittersweet this meeting was—how I'd missed my father, but would give anything to instead be back in Rio's arms. I didn't deserve happiness when I'd just seen a rosary hung on my lover's door.

"Papa…"

He held me, seeming to understand at least a little of what I'd been through. "I am so very sorry I couldn't make the changes you wanted to see happen. I wish I could have, Bella," he said, pulling away from me to gaze into my eyes. "Things here are not what they should be. You know that. And I didn't realize how bad it really was until I saw you at the prison. Until I tried to do what you asked and saw how far-reaching the problem was."

I didn't want to cry in front of him. I didn't want to cry at all, but I was awfully close. "It's okay, Papa. I appreciate that you tried. But, Rio—they're going to kill him." I hadn't allowed myself to think the words until now. To let my mind grasp the import of those rosary beads on his door. But now… now…

I burst into tears, collapsing into my father's shoulders.

He patted me awkwardly on the back. "Your mother was always so much better at this. Don't cry."

When I had calmed, he continued. "So, Rio. The man you talked about?"

I nodded silently.

His next words were careful. "Child, Gateau has told me some things about him. Things that aren't very pleasant."

Gateau. I wanted to spit the word, then stomp it into the ground. The thought of him left an unpleasant taste in my mouth. He'd rescued me, but sentenced Rio to death. "Rio doesn't deserve what's happening to him. Gateau had photos, but I just can't believe he'd do that. We need more

201

time. Something's not right. They're going to kill him next week."

He lifted a hand to my shoulder and gave it a squeeze. "I'm not saying we have to give up, Bella, but I'm not sure we have many options left. I've lost a lot of my political power due to these bribery charges."

"Gateau…"

"Gateau is the only reason I'm not in jail," my father said firmly. "Without his support, I'd be in el Castillo myself."

I didn't know how to answer that. Something about this said that it was all Gateau's fault, if only I could connect the dots.

He gave me one last pat on the shoulder, as if reassuring himself that I was truly there with him, or perhaps reminding me that things were different than they had been just an hour earlier. "Get some sleep, my flower. We'll work on this some more tomorrow."

I walked upstairs and stepped into the shower, a zombie. The water was hot enough to make me flinch, and to leave my skin red and raw.

I washed my hair twice. And then I stood in the stream of water until it grew cold. For how many nights had I dreamed about a shower? And now here I was, willing to trade it back for just one more night with Rio.

The sheets in my bed smelled like sunshine and grass. The smoothness felt wrong on my skin, after the rough cotton I'd become used to. The bed was too big, and too soft.

And too empty.

34: RIO

I was alone. I was hungry, but I didn't complain. Why bother? I'd be dead soon. I could go hungry for seven more days.

I'd stopped pacing when Diego came to gloat. Stopped doing anything but waiting for it all to end. He must have called up a favor from the guards, I didn't think anyone was allowed to see me.

I remained where I was, crouched with my arms around my knees in a corner beside a thick, rusted pipe, waiting for the insults to start.

"El Lobo."

"Fuck off." My words sounded tired, even to my own ears.

Silence, then, "You were a worthy adversary."

I looked up. It wasn't like Diego to spin macho bullshit when he could kick a man instead. His face, beyond the dark iron bars of my cell, was troubled. I licked my lips, forcing moisture back into them. "What do you want?"

"I... don't know." He attempted a scowl. "Perhaps I just wanted to gloat."

I shrugged, arms not leaving my wrapped legs. "Well, here I am. Gloat away."

"Aren't you going to get angry? To rage against the injustice of it all?"

I answered with a question. "What are you doing time for, Diego—in el Castillo, that is? Robbery? Murder?"

He grinned, showing yellow teeth. This at least, was familiar ground. "I killed the fucker who tried to rape my mom," he sneered. "Dad deserved everything he got."

My smile didn't reach my eyes. Why bother when there was no emotion left inside? "They say I killed 23 people."

He stood back. Silence filled the cell again. Then, "Did you?"

"It doesn't matter now, does it? At the time though, I thought I'd do anything for love." I licked my lips again. I'd never said this to anyone before, but... I would die soon. It would be good to get it off my chest. "You ask why I'm not angry. I've tried that. For all the years that I've been here. The rage fed me, sustained me when all I wanted to do was die."

I looked up at him. "But in the end, nothing changed. What's the point? They all still leave. Whether by choice or circumstance, it makes no difference in the end."

Diego looked at his shoes, then the wall, then eventually at his hands. I sat in silence, waiting for him to get to the real reason for his visit. "Gateau," Diego said, after so long I'd thought he would turn and leave. "He's fucked up, eh? A *loco gringo*."

I didn't say anything. Just sat there, with my arms wrapped around me on the ground.

Diego scratched at the tattoo of the Razor on his arm. "I didn't know he was going to give you the Rosario," he said eventually.

"What does it matter?" I said quietly. "You wanted me dead."

"Not like this, el Lobo. We both know the charges against you are wrong." Diego grimaced, then turned and headed for the door. Before he got there, he spun back once more. "I wanted you dead, yes, but by my own hands, in a fair fight," he said. "Not hanging from the length of a rope, a broken man. It just feels wrong."

35: BELLA

I woke to find that I had been dreaming about Rio's tattoos. One, in particular—a backwards 'Love' which covered up a scar. *She's the reason I'm here. I thought I loved her. She didn't love me.*

Could he have been referring to the bank robbery?

With sudden curiosity, I pulled my laptop over; balancing it on my knees as I sat up in bed. The incident wasn't hard to find. 23 people dead, just as Gateau claimed, including five tellers, the bank manager, and one infant. I read the article quickly, my mouth dropping lower and lower with each new horrific line:

CITY SHOCKED BY ROBBERY GONE WRONG

Rio Ruíz, the softly spoken man behind last year's Gibson Heist disaster was imprisoned today on 23 counts of murder.

The skinny 18-year-old local boy will spend his life behind bars after a special court found him guilty on all charges in a closed session.

The case is not without its controversy. His accomplice, Miss Elizabeth Kilroy, English, 25, will walk away with only a 6-month suspended sentence. Originally tried alongside Ruíz, and suspected by many commentators of being the actual shooter, the case took a dramatic turn when Ruíz made a statement saying that he had held the gun.

Without video evidence to back them up, and with no witnesses left alive, it is said that frustrated prosecutors asked him if he knew the impact of his words.

"I'd do anything for love," was his reply.

Miss Kilroy was asked for comments as she left the courtroom a free woman.

"It is with deep regret that I allowed myself to be caught up with Rio Ruíz," she said in a prepared statement. "My heart goes out to the families of the victims, even those of the bank manager with who, as you all know from the court case, I'd been having difficulties. I feel vindicated by the decision of this court to clear me of all murder charges. Hopefully the rumors that the gun belonged to me can now finally be put to rest. Rio is a fool of a man. He got exactly what he deserved."

When asked if she would visit her ex-lover in prison, Miss Kilroy just laughed and walked away.

36: RIO

Gateau came to visit on the sixth morning. I'd known he would—the chance to gloat over his captive was too good a chance to pass up. His footsteps clunked on the cold concrete floor, echoing down through the cells ahead of me and announcing his arrival.

"*El Lobo,*" he said, his voice stating in no uncertain terms what he thought of the name. He chuckled. "Less *wolf* now, I think, and more *my little bitch!*"

I didn't look up from my corner. I'd been shivering before he arrived. I fought to stop it now.

His shoes—polished black leather—kicked the bars of my cell, making it ring. "One more night, el Lobo. You can thank the Warden for that—if it was up to me, I'd kill you right now." He sighed, as if he carried the weight of the world on his shoulders. "I guess I can see his point— gunshots play hell with organ transplants. A heart's no good with a hole in it."

My only response was a growl.

"You know, the organ angle is a new thing. The Warden and I, we figured that prostitution just wasn't enough."

This time I ignored him completely. I wondered if there was some way I could damage my own organs, before my death, so they couldn't be used.

He tapped at the bars idly. "It's strange, but I'd thought I'd enjoy this little visit. Now that I'm here though, you're really just rather pathetic." He smirked. "It's like watching a tiger in a pen, but one without any teeth or claws." He kicked the bars again with his foot. "Enjoy your final night, *friend*. The one thing you won't be enjoying is Bella. She's at home, probably forgotten all about you."

His fingers tapped on his chin. He looked at me from the corner of his eyes. "You know, maybe I'll pay her a visit. Ask her out to dinner tonight. Since I'm responsible for her release, you can bet she'll be feeling appreciative."

My eyes narrowed.

He laughed, noticing my reaction. He rocked his hips for emphasis, tipping up to the balls of his shoes, then back. "Appreciative indeed. I know exactly what I'll be having for dessert."

I growled.

He leaned forward. "In case you missed the subtle reference…" His teeth bared, "That means I'm going to *fuck* her."

I leapt to my feet, surging forward against the bars with a roar. I lunged at him through the iron. "I'll kill you!" It was bad enough to be in here. It was bad enough to know what would come. "I'll fucking kill you!"

He laughed, stepping back out of my reach. "So the tiger has claws after all," he chuckled, then made a motion as if tipping a hat. "Well, not for long."

I strained against the bars, the Red back with such force it was the only thing I could see. I'd pound his face to pulp. Tear him apart piece by piece. But as strong as I was, the bars refused to bend.

Gateau laughed. "Nice knowing you, *el Lobo*." He turned and moved down the hall. "I'm off to dinner."

Soon the only sounds in the cell were the echoes of his casual laughter, and my incoherent roars.

37: BELLA

For six days, the ticking clock on the wall had mocked me. I'd leapt out of bed that first morning, calling for my father, but when I'd showed him the article, he'd just frowned and said it made the situation even worse. "He's a mass murderer, my flower. I understand you have feelings for him, but this all looks pretty clear."

"Can't you see! He took the blame!"

"That's not what this article says."

"Papa. You must believe me. If mama was alive and in trouble, would you take the blame for her?"

Papa nodded, frowning.

"This is just the same! Even the prosecutors thought she did it, they just couldn't prove anything."

"Maybe. But..."

I seized his hands. "Papa. I know Rio. You've heard me talk about him. Does he seem dangerous?"

He cleared his throat. "Well... actually yes. He's seven-foot-tall, wider than an ox and covered in tattoos. Yes, he does."

I thought about that. "Okay. Maybe those were the wrong words. Papa, he saved me, when I was in prison."

"I'm sure that's what you think-"

I shook my head. I'd wanted to spare him the details, but… "They were going to rape me, Papa. I was on the bed, they were holding me down, and one of them was undoing their pants. Rio saved me. He saved your daughter."

Papa's face went white. He stumbled on his words for a long minute. "They…"

I nodded. "Rio saved me," I said softly. "He's the kindest, sweetest man I know. When he gets angry, it's to protect something he loves. 237 people live in safety because of him, free from drugs and gang violence. I'm alive because of *him*, Papa. He wouldn't kill all those innocent people. I know it."

My father's white, bushy brows furrowed. Eventually, he nodded once. "I believe you."

"You do?"

"You're my daughter. Every time I look at you, I see your mother in your eyes. You wouldn't lie, not about this. I believe you."

Despite my father's assurances that he believed me, there was little that could be done. The clock ticked louder every hour. He made phone calls, day after day, but they had no effect. He called meetings, but no one came. It seemed that word had been spread that he was caught up in a bribery investigation. Nobody wanted to come close.

For my own part, I called every person I knew, and I tried the local newspaper, and the police station, and the mayor. Everyone had either been bought, or was disinterested, or didn't have time for a little rich girl's whines about a prisoner on death row. When I tried to leave the house, to argue my case in person, or perhaps sneak back into prison, I discovered that a guard had been posted to follow my every move.

My father just smiled sadly when I accused him. "My flower, I'm sorry for your loss. But I can't afford to lose you too."

And still I'd had no sign of Gateau. The swine. The pig that'd put my lover on death row.

Until, on the sixth day, he knocked upon my door.

He stood on the other side, freshly groomed and pressed. "Bella." His smile, fake and overpowering, was splashed upon his face like cologne.

I fought the urge to slam the door in his face. "Gateau," I said flatly. "What are you doing here?"

"Stopping by to see how you are, of course. And to tell you I'll be by this evening to pick you up for dinner. I do believe we have a little bit of celebrating to do. I'm in the mood for dessert."

A heavy lump formed in my throat. I had nothing to celebrate, and certainly not with Gateau. If it were up to me, I'd choose to never see his face again.

"I don't think I'll be available this evening," I said, beginning to push the door closed.

He reached out to intercept the door, leaning into it and crossing the threshold. "Now, you know I'm not one to take no for an answer. I'll be here at seven."

He brought his hand to his forehead as if tipping an invisible hat, the watch at his wrist catching the morning sunlight, then turned and sauntered toward the compound's exit.

38: RIO

I slammed my body against the bars with a roar, then grabbed them with my fists and shook them for the hundredth time. I'd been pounding the metal since Gateau left. My fists were bloody and my body bruised, but the rage kept me strong. Rage at Gateau. Rage at what he'd said he would do to Bella.

I couldn't believe she would fall for it. I had to believe she was stronger and smarter than that. But a man that ran a prostitution ring and drugged women to do his bidding wouldn't be afraid of doing the same with her, if she resisted him.

My hand slammed into the bars once again. The sound echoed off the walls, filling the small space, but I didn't care. Let the guards hear my roars. Let the whole prison hear my rage.

In fury, I strode to the metal piping that adorned one wall. I wanted to destroy something—break this prison apart. It was bolted down and should have been too secure to move. But when I worked my fingers around it and heaved, a section came away in my hands.

I bellowed as I smashed it against the iron, the sound now incredibly loud. Over and over, until the pipe bent. And still I didn't stop.

…Until a faint tapping echoed through the cell— unusual, because it was the first noise that I hadn't made. It cut through the anger. Like a confused beast, I paused; my head cocked. *The tapping had a pattern*. My rage dimmed as I listened to the sound. One soft rap. One loud rap. Three soft raps. Three loud raps. Over and over again.

I searched for the source of the noise, and eventually found it in the sister pipe beside the one I'd broken. I rushed to the back wall, placing my hands against the metal tubing still bolted there. It vibrated as sound travelled down it from above.

That was Morse Code! Tentatively, I tapped a response. *'Mateo?'*

One soft rap. One loud rap. Three soft raps. Three loud raps. *'Rio.'*

'What are you doing?'

'Mama says we have to help.'

'You're a good boy. But there's nothing you can do.'

His message took a long time coming, tapped out painstakingly on the pipe in his room. *'Mama says you're going away. What does that mean, Rio?'*

My eyes closed, the anger now fully gone. It was a while before I could tap a response. *'It means you need to stick together now—all of you. To be strong.'*

'Even the gangs and the bad people?'

I nodded to myself. Even the bad people. *'Tell your mama to gather everyone in the courtyard.'* Too few watched the killings anymore. Maybe if they gathered, my death would be useful. It would shock them. It would goad them into giving up their feuds; force them to protect each other.

When we were done, I leaned back against the wall. So many people to care for. It wasn't 237 anymore. That was where I'd always been wrong. There were over 700 in the prison. I feared for them, when I was gone.

39: BELLA

When Gateau arrived promptly at seven—the same gun he'd used to threaten Rio sitting arrogantly on his hip—I still wore the same jeans and button up top I'd worn earlier, my hair tossed up carelessly. I stared mutely at him from across the open door.

"Well," Gateau said as he assessed me. I could hear the censure in his voice. "Running behind, are you?"

"Nope," I snapped. "This is as good as it gets."

Gateau gave a little shrug, like he was absolving me of sin. He gestured for me to step out onto the porch. "Let's go, then. The cantina awaits."

I followed him reluctantly out of the house. I'd wanted to be strong—to tell him he could get lost. But the appeal of hearing something about Rio, the unrealistic fantasy of hearing things had changed back at the prison, outweighed my best intentions.

But that didn't mean I had to be pleasant. I trailed along sullenly, kicking at the dust as we went, imagining it settling into his socks and irritating his skin.

We sat at the same little table we'd eaten at before, and just like then, Gateau ordered food for us both without consulting me first.

He poured me a glass of wine I didn't want and had no intention of drinking, and one for himself as well. Then he tipped the glass toward mine, letting it clink against the rim. "Here's to your fortuitous escape."

I said nothing in return.

"Now, now, Bella. I can tell you're still thinking of that Rio. You mustn't waste your time on him any longer. He's getting exactly what he deserves. Those pictures I showed you were just the tip of the iceberg, really. You can't imagine the grief and suffering he's brought to others. It would only be a matter of time before he brought that to you, as well."

"I can't really speak to that, Gateau," I said primly. "I know nothing about the bank robbery. I know very little at all about Rio prior to his time at the prison." I adjusted the silverware, waiting for Gateau to fill the silence. When he didn't, I decided to poke at his words. "What I do know is that Rio has been kind and generous to me, and there are others who think highly of him. Two hundred and thirty-seven people, to be exact. Conditions in prison are terrible, Gateau. For a start, there's-"

He raised a hand to forestall further lectures. "Let's not be dramatic." His words and tone were dismissive. "I know your experience in the prison wasn't a good one—how could it be? And I think the trauma of the whole thing is coloring your perspective." He smiled in what I was sure he meant to be a non-condescending manner. "I know all about the two hundred and thirty-seven people in *el Loco's* quadrant. He thinks himself a god looking over them. They'll be better off when he's gone."

I ignored his tone, focusing instead on the words. "How do you know all this stuff about the prison?" I asked, frowning. Gateau seemed to know an awful lot. "For that matter, how did you get into the prison to rescue me with no guards, the other night?" My eyes narrowed. "Did you use the Apex? How did you know about that?"

He shifted uncomfortably. He'd met me in the Apex, that time he'd left me in prison. He couldn't lie about it now. "Of course."

"So, the men who visit the prostitutes with the prison's permission—that's common knowledge, then?" A horrible thought occurred to me. "You're not… one of them, are you?"

Gateau blanched. "Of course not. Most of those women are filthy natives." He reached across the table, taking me by my creamy white hand. "I have much finer tastes."

I pulled my hand back. *Filthy natives?* He was talking about Ezzi, a woman who was my friend! "So you knew about the prostitution ring, but chose to do nothing about it."

"Well," he said, pausing to press a linen napkin to his mouth. "I'm not sure I would call the ring common knowledge, exactly, but it is well known among the higher ups that it happens."

"Interesting. But the guards who allow it to happen aren't reprimanded for-"

Gateau's hand smacked down on the table. The plates jumped and red wine sloshed over the side of my glass. He took a deep breath, visibly controlling his temper. "Come now, Bella, I think you might be in a little over your head, here." He reached for a napkin to mop at the spilled wine. "You know nothing about the inner workings of the prison, or how things happen here in this country. Perhaps you should take a step back instead of being a spoiled troublemaker meddling in everyone else's affairs."

He acted as if he was in charge, or something! His gold watch glinted as he worked the paper napkin against the linen of the table.

Watching it, a horrible suspicion formed in my mind. You'd need someone on the outside to organize the clients for the ring, wouldn't you? Preferably someone with government connections, to clean up any messes that were spilled?

Suddenly, I knew where I'd seen that watch before.

"And what is your affiliation with the prison?" I said, sounding him out. "If you ask me, the whole thing should be burned to the ground."

"Really?" Gateau said, eyes narrowed. "Weren't you just trying to protect it?"

I shook my head, my eyes going to his gold watch once more. The same watch the Razors had taken when I first came to prison. "I thought so, at first. But then you showed me those photos."

I swallowed. Forcing the next words out—trying not to think of the meaning behind them. "Anyone that did that, deserves his fate." Gateau was the key here. He had a way in and out of the prison. The beginnings of a plan were starting to form, but first, I had to get him to trust me.

An eyebrow rose. He played with his knife, tapping it idly on the table. "What do you think about the prostitution ring, then?"

"Well it's not for me," I said, thinking quickly. I'd have to be subtle about this. "Though I believe that every woman should be able to choose what she wants to do with her body, and that means prostitution is okay."

He nodded, eyes still narrowed.

"But!" I said, holding up a hand, "drugging those women is wrong." I swallowed, praying I had the strength to say the next words. "Even if, you know, if they're…" I looked left and right, the words feeling wrong, but necessary. I lowered my voice. "…colored."

I could tell, to the second, the moment that Gateau relaxed. The creases on his forehead disappeared. His shoulders lowered. The corners of his face curled up into a smile.

"You know, I have some small amount of power at the prison," he said suddenly. "Especially with regards to the women." It was as if we were talking about the weather. "Perhaps there's a better way to approach things. Maybe we should discuss it, later, over drinks at my place? I'd be happy to pass on your ideas to the appropriate authorities."

He must think me an idiot. To even try that line on me said so much about his arrogance, his personality, his casual racism, his contempt for women and for me. I opened my mouth to snap back at him, but closed it silently a moment later. I was careful not to let my real thoughts show on my face.

No matter how horrified I was at his casual attitude toward prostitution, drugs, or even sentencing someone to death, Gateau was a powerbroker in the prison—perhaps, I was starting to realize, even the man at the very top. Rio had learned to control his anger. Now it was my turn to control my hate.

I leaned in. "Can I tell you a secret, Gateau?" I needed him to trust me. To get me back inside the prison, before it was too late.

His eyes flicked down to my cleavage, then back up at me. I fought the urge to pull my top higher as he licked his lips and nodded. "Please."

"I'm glad Rio is dying. Is that wrong?"

He shook his head. "Not at all. I feel the same way." He cast me a sideways glance. "You didn't hear it from me, but there's more of that to come, too."

I squeezed my elbows slightly together on the table. "Really?"

Gateau's eyes flicked down to my cleavage again. He nodded. "Diego. I'm told he's the ringleader of the prostitution ring. Much more powerful than he seems." He watched me under hooded lids for my reaction.

"Good," I said, letting all the hatred I felt for the man swell up. *Controlled hate. Let it out only when it was appropriate.* "The entire gang can rot in hell for what they tried to do to me."

The words had the desired effect. Gateau grinned. "Most of the gang will join him, after, truthfully. They're all filthy criminals. The world will be better without them."

"That sounds like a start, then," I said, feeling out the words. If I imagined Gateau as the one on the gallows, I found I could tell the lie convincingly. "I suppose we have you to thank for that?"

He preened, relaxing. "I don't like to blow my own horn, but, you know…" he winked.

I filled his wine glass and offered him a smile. "You're so brave," I murmured. This time, the words were more of a struggle. There was a sour taste at the back of my mouth when I said them. I seized my wine glass, filled it as well, and downed the contents in one gulp.

He took me for an idiot, saying I was only a woman. I'd play both assumptions to my advantage. "So, my brave hero who rescued me from prison. Tell me about yourself."

It was all I had to say.

Over dinner, Gateau talked about nothing but himself. I pushed and prodded at my food, murmuring at all the right times, refilling his glass whenever I could. When they cleared the table, they took three empty bottles of wine with them. We'd both had a lot to drink.

Gateau stood, offering me his arm. "Shall we?"

I leapt up in feigned excitement. Gateau would journey to the prison tomorrow, to gloat over Rio's execution. Over dinner, I'd formed a plan.

Get his trust. Get his gun. Get my ticket back to el Castillo.

It wasn't much, but it was a start. The trust, I was reasonably confident I had. My sweet talking—or was that hate talking—over dinner had won him over. I might even be able to accompany him without suspicion.

But a way to grab his gun had proved more difficult. The solution had come to me when I'd noticed him licking his lips and staring at my breasts for what seemed the fiftieth time.

"Thank you so much for dinner," I murmured, letting my body brush up against his as we stepped out into the night. I tipped my head back, hoping I looked adoring. "And for everything you've been doing at the prison as well."

He looked towards me. "Perhaps we should make a little detour by my place on the way home. Stop off and have *dessert*."

I swallowed, then smiled and nodded. Ezzi had done it for the sake of her child. Now I would do it for the sake of my man. I'd do anything to save Rio's life. Even be a prostitute for the night.

40: BELLA

Gateau pulled a set of keys from his pocket when he stepped up to his two-story house. I didn't miss the fact that he locked the deadbolt behind me after we walked inside.

Get his trust. Get his gun. Get my ticket back to el Castillo. I repeated the words to myself like a mantra. Somehow, if I could attain all three, I could fix this. It was crazy, I knew. But Rio had put everything on the line for me. Now it was my turn to do the same.

I pulled my hair down from its ponytail, shaking it out so it fell in a thick mass down my back.

"This look suits you, Bella." He stepped close, wrapping a curl around his finger.

I repressed a shiver. Then I tipped back my head like I couldn't wait for his next touch.

He poured us both more wine. "Why don't we drink this in the bedroom?"

I followed him up the stairs.

His room was just as I'd imagined—a seedy four-poster bed with red velvet drapes and an overly large mirror on the wall. But it was also somehow sterile—everything was obsessively neat: the sheets had ironed creases and every surface and shelf was bare. The only personal item out of place was a single bottle of aftershave, placed exactly in the center of the bedside table.

I perched on its edge, eyeing the gun on Gateau's hip.

There had to be another way to do this. I could knock him out—hit him with a vase, seize the gun and run. But... I needed him, tomorrow, to get into the prison.

I could say I was tired, suggest we meet tomorrow. But then I wouldn't get the gun. It seemed I could get either the gun or entry to el Castillo without going any further, but to get both? Well, that was why I was sitting on his bed.

And I needed both. Gateau could get me into the execution—give me a reason to be in the courtyard, tomorrow. When I got there, I would need the gun to stop it from going ahead.

I looked up at Gateau, as he stood above me. He was looking down my top. "Why don't you come and sit on the bed beside me?" I said, patting the duvet.

He sat. If Ezzi could do this, I could too.

I started working on the buttons of my blouse. His eyes widened.

"Well? I asked. "Aren't you going to take off your shirt?"

He scrabbled at his buttons. He pulled his shirt off to reveal a pasty white chest.

I could do this. For Rio, I could do this.

I'd imagined maybe, if I thought of Rio, I might fool myself into thinking it was him. I knew as soon as Gateau kissed me that I was wrong. Our teeth clashed. His tongue probed at me like an octopus.

I could do this. For Rio.

I eyed his belt, letting him chew at my face like a slobbering dog. I needed to get the belt off, get the gun, and then get out of here. My fingers went for the buckle.

"My, aren't you keen?"

"I thought we could have dessert."

He chuckled, like I'd just said something funny, then lay back. "So, we're going to do it?"

I shook my head. I'd known the question was coming. Already planned my answer. "Not on the first date. But... I want to do something to show you how much I appreciate your saving me."

My hands pulled down his pants, resting his gun and holster on the bedside table. Then I grit my teeth and slipped my fingers beneath the fabric of his shorts.

Rio fought for me. This is my version of doing the same.

Compared to Rio, Gateau was... laughable. Fully extended, he barely fit in the palm of my hand. A few short strokes and he was gasping, ready for completion. I paused on the vinegar stroke.

His eyes went wide. His pelvis tried to buck under my hands. "Why'd you stop?"

In his own way, it was Rio who had taught me the power of the pause. "You know Gateau, I'm so grateful that you saved me from that beast."

"Yes, yes. Whatever," he gasped. He looked meaningfully at my hand. "I'm sure there's a way you can thank me."

"I was just thinking. Could I come to the execution tomorrow? Would you take me?"

He hips ground upon the bed, thrusting. "I don't know, Bella," he said, his mind on other things. "It's... um... it's not a pretty sight."

I stroked him a couple more times, with thumb and forefinger. Then my hand fell away. "I'd just like some... *completion*. Don't you think that would be nice?"

His eyes bugged out. "Whatever. Anything." He tried to grind against me again.

I began to stroke slowly. "You really mean that?" I asked in my best bimbo voice. "I'd be ever so happy."

He nodded, eyes never leaving my hand.

"Great!" I said, speeding up. "I'll be round here first thing tomorrow morning."

I slipped my hand away as soon as he cried out. I pretended to cough as spasms shook, and he coated his own body.

"Oh, darling," Gateau said, when it was over. Sleepiness was already sinking into his voice. "I didn't know you had that in you."

I smiled, looking away. I'd done so much I didn't think I'd have the strength to do tonight. "Neither did I."

Moments later, he fell into slumber. I sat there, for a time, on the bedspread. I'd thought I'd feel shame, after what I'd done. I'd thought I'd feel dirty, and a whore, and impure.

I pulled the gun from the bedside table, popping it into my bag. I threw the holster under the bed. But for five days I'd sat in my room, impotent. Now, finally doing something to save the man I loved, I felt… strong.

41: BELLA

It was a shaky plan. Last night, I'd focused only on getting into the prison and getting a gun. But now, after sleeping on the floor in my room—my bed was still too soft—the plan had grown and evolved. I had a gun now. I had friends on the inside. And I had enemies. *I would use all three to my advantage.*

I braided my hair—the way I knew Rio liked it—and picked out a floral skirt and white peasant top I thought might distract Gateau. Then I wrote three notes. One to Lumen, one to Diego, and one to father. The note for Papa, I left sitting on his desk. He would find it when he sat down to start work for the day, too late to stop me. The note for Lumen, I hoped to give to him, if I could, in prison. I'd need his help spreading the word about what I wanted to do.

The note for Diego… I didn't know if I could get him my note, or even if he would read it. But Gateau had said the next rosary would be for him. And maybe, just maybe, the enemy of my enemy could also be my friend.

Gateau had a smug grin on his face and a lump in his pants when I answered the door. My thoughts flicked briefly back to last night, but I had no regrets. What did my body matter when Rio was about to lose his?

Still, *gracias a Dios* that Papa was there, behind me, shaking Gateau's hand and then waving goodbye. It gave me the excuse to fob him off when we got in the chauffeured car. "Papa just kissed me goodbye," I explained when the inevitable question came. "Let's wait until we get back."

We arrived at the prison prior to the execution. There was no pat down, there were no security measures. I was Gateau's special guest, and no one questioned my attendance. If I hadn't thought he was involved before, now I knew for certain. Every guard we met was in on this thing with him. I could tell in the way they grinned and shook his hand as he walked past—like he'd just bought their family Christmas dinner.

Gateau and his guards led us straight through the main entrance. We exited into the courtyard the same way I'd first arrived—through the guardhouse that ran the length of the three massive front gates in bullet proof glass; two of them closed, the middle ones—huge blast doors that would lock down permanently if something went wrong—open.

When we stepped onto the dirt and crossed the courtyard I spotted Lumen, propped up against the wall nearby. At his side was Ezzi and her young son.

When Lumen spotted me, his eyes widened in surprise. I let a rush of people separate Gateau from me, then bumped into him as I walked past. I pressed the note into his hand, giving it the faintest squeeze. Then I stepped back into the wave of people.

Last time, the courtyard had been empty.

This time, it teemed with life. Maybe it had been the recent upheaval; the unsettling changes that had been taking place. Or maybe it was just that people knew and loved Rio. They filled the little space.

His enemies were also there. The Razors patrolled the area—I'd thought they would strut like proud hounds at the prospect of *el Lobo's* impending death, but they patrolled quietly, respectfully. Almost… regretfully. Diego gave a start when he saw me, eyes narrowing, and scowled. Instead of returning it, I beckoned him closer, behind Gateau's back.

Surprisingly, he did as I requested, moving closer through the crowd. When he got close enough, I put my finger to my lips, looking at Gateau, and pressed the note into his hand. His eyes narrowed at the touch of crumpled paper, and he opened his mouth to spit back a reply. Before he could, I looked him squarely in the eye and reached into my purse, pressing the gun into his hand.

It was a leap of faith, but then this whole day was. Diego might not want to save Rio, but he sure as hell would want to save himself. The gun was both a token of my goodwill, to show I was genuine, and a means by which he might act.

He appraised me for one long moment, his gaze lingering on the unspoken plea on my lips, then moved back away from me with a thoughtful look on his face, to be swallowed by the crowd.

Get Gateau's trust. Get his gun. Get my ticket back to el Castillo. I'd done all three now. Silently, I said a prayer to myself. And hoped I hadn't come to watch Rio's body drop and sway in the cold wind of the courtyard.

42: RIO

Over the last seven days I had imagined a hundred ways I could avoid this end.

Sometimes I thought of a great escape, over the walls and away from this place forever. Bella would be at my side. We'd go south, somewhere in South America, live next to a beach and make love all day.

And other times, I dreamed only of beating Gateau to the punch. If I had to be dead and gone, at least I could do it on my own terms. At least I would be able to take that victory away from him.

But I hadn't, of course. I'd thought I was broken, till Gateau came to visit. After that, the rage had kept me alive. Rage at him, and what he'd threatened. Rage at myself, and those three little words that, the last time I'd seen Bella, I hadn't had the courage to say.

The rage simmered now, a low growl that had scared away the first two guards that came to collect me, until eventually they returned with four more. They'd tried to pull me from the cell. Pleaded with me to make it easy for them. But I wasn't going easy. I'd stood in that doorway, muscles bunched, and called them in for a fight.

They'd levelled guns at me. I'd laughed them off, leaping at my bars to rattle my cage. Did they think threatening to kill me before my execution would work? All four had left after a hurried discussion. The next time they returned there were 12 of them. They must have pulled them in from the walls.

Every single one was dressed in riot gear. I took down five before they got cuffs on me. Another two before they shackled my feet and pushed me forward. I fought them still, ineffectively, all the way out into the yard.

Ezzi stood to one side of the main gate, next to Diego, when I was paraded past. So many people in the courtyard, to watch my death. I stopped fighting, standing tall. My death should have a purpose, after all.

The guards pulled me toward the gallows. The crowds parted as we went, their chatter becoming hushed. Some looked away. Others were openly staring.

I kept my head high. I wouldn't let them see me defeated. I had spent too much time being *el Lobo*. It was the only legacy I had to give.

I stepped up onto the stairs and across the platform. The guards fell away one by one as I did, until it was just one man with his hand on my shoulder, and another waiting for me beside the lever that would be my end.

The noose went over my head, loose at first, then tighter, the knot carefully placed. I looked out over the crowd, focusing on the faces I knew. Memorizing the feel of the sun on my face. I found myself smiling, despite my impending death. I had a clock tattooed on my shoulder, the numbers running backwards. But if I could do it all again, I would, just for those final weeks I'd had with *her*.

She'd taught me so much. How to feel again. How to be human. *How to love*.

And now my eyes did glisten. Not in fear, but in regret for what I hadn't said. If she were here right now, I tell her… I'd tell her…

She was here right now.

My breath hitched. Impossible. But no, there she was, tucked against the far wall, her dark hair in a braid and worry etched into her face. God's last gift to me, an angel sent to bless my demise.

I didn't question the gift. I could hear the guards moving even now—at any moment it would be too late. Our eyes connected, and my mouth opened. Though none could hear it, I whispered the words that would let me die happy.

"I love you."

43: BELLA

His lips moved, and all the distance in the world didn't stop me from hearing them. My heart soared as I basked for the briefest instant in the glow of three simple, little words.

But... all those words would mean nothing if Rio died. I forced myself down from the high his lips had created, taking stock of the situation at hand. Rio's death was just moments away.

I locked eyes with Rio again, and he was smiling — finally at peace. But I wasn't. My eyes flicked urgently to the guard at Rio's side. Then back to him. Then to the guard again as I tried to signal Rio.

He frowned, the smile faltering. Then looked to where I had indicated just as a ripple ran through the crowd — a murmur that picked up like a breeze over water, of agitated voices and then urgent cries.

There was a commotion at the front, just before the stage. The guards at the bottom of the stairs ran to investigate. The cries from the crowd grew louder and louder and then the guards *disappeared*, sucked into a maelstrom of angry people.

I'd had a conversation with Rio about it once. *It's like the guards, right? There are 20 times as many men in Diego's gang as there are law enforcement. The guards need to rule by fear. If they didn't, they wouldn't have a chance.*

Diego leapt to the stage, holding his weapon to the head of the guard who stood beside Rio. *Strange, how fearless you could get with a gun in your hand and the knowledge that you'd been scheduled to die.*

Across the courtyard, guards found themselves suddenly surrounded by angry Razors. The guard on stage held up his hands as chanting began to echo from the courtyard walls. Diego plucked the gun from his holster, and Razors all throughout the prison finally realized what outnumbering the guards 20-to-1 actually meant.

My heart soared. *We were doing it!* The chanting reached a crescendo and the entire prison devolved into a riot. The crowd surged forward, arming themselves with the guard's own weapons. Diego strode across the stage to Rio.

The cry of triumph faltered on my lips, as I realized, for the briefest of moments, that I'd given Diego his freedom, but that didn't mean he would give Rio his. He could just as easily walk to the lever, and pull it, as loosen the noose.

Diego looked at me, as if realizing the same thing I did. But then he shook his head, and I swear I saw him mouth *enemy of my enemy* as he removed the noose from Rio's neck.

I ran toward Rio, through the rioting crowd.

Gateau ran the other way, toward the exit.

44: RIO

"Enemy of my enemy," Diego muttered.

I just stood there, too stunned to move. "Diego. You're rescuing me?"

The noose went slack around my neck, and then Diego forced the guard to unlock the cuffs that bound me.

"You'll never get away from this," the guard muttered.

I laughed, euphoria sweeping over me. I imagined I was in one of the old Spanish crime movies I'd watched as a child.

"The Warden will find you, and then you'll all end up wearing rosary beads, you filthy, scum sucking-"

The guard crumpled to the ground as Diego answered his insults with the butt of his gun to a temple. "Let's go," Diego growled, flicking me a glance. "I'll see my men safe, and then be right behind you."

I moved toward the edge of the stage.

"Rio?"

"Yes," I said, pausing.

"Tell your woman thanks."

I nodded and leaped from the platform into the sea of people, forcing a path to Bella as she fought her way to the gallows.

"Bella!" I met her with a kiss, and for one long moment the crowds, the riot, the danger we were still in, faded away as two souls met and became one. I'd do anything for this woman. And she'd proven she would do the same.

When we broke, she gestured toward the main entrance. "It's not over yet. We need to get out of here. Diego bought us your life, and Lumen bought us time with this riot, but if we can't force the gate before the guards recover and start to shut the place down, we'll be fish in a barrel. They can pick us off from the outside."

I didn't stop to say anything, just took her arm and started running. She matched me step for step. Lumen pushed his way through the crowd too, carrying Mateo in his arms. I plucked the small, frightened child from him, then used my bulk to clear a path for all four of us toward the exit.

The sharp retort of a gun rang out behind us. We could force the inner gate with enough people, but if the guards panicked and those blast doors came down, we'd never be able to leave. Our only chance was to get there before they realized what was happening. Thank goodness so many of them had left the walls to escort me inside.

Up ahead a familiar outline reached the guard post at the main gate. Patented black leather shoes and a gold watch flashed as he hammered on the door. "Gateau," I growled, doubling my speed. If he got inside, he wouldn't care about those still trapped here. He'd slam those blast doors closed and leave us all to our fate.

The guardhouse doors opened just as we arrived, Gateau slipping through and slamming it behind him as my fingers stretched uselessly toward it. We were seconds too late.

Diego arrived with his men as my fists pounded uselessly on reinforced metal and glass. "That's it then," I said to the world at large. "It was a nice try, but we failed."

"Can we bust through the guardhouse?" Diego asked, panting, cocking his gun.

I shook my head. "It's bullet proof glass. We can't even shoot our way through. We're done." I turned to Bella. "It was a good try, *gata salvaje*. It was worth it to see your face again."

Strangely, Bella didn't seem as disappointed as I felt. With all our plans crashing down around us, she still found time to glace at Lumen at smile. "Do you think she made it?"

Lumen shrugged. "She's the only one that could try—if we were ever going to pray that they'd take up the offer of free sex, lets pray it happens now."

"What on earth are you talking about?" demanded Diego.

I glanced to the child in my arms. And suddenly realized we were missing one from our party.

45: BELLA

Gateau laughed at us through the glass, reveling in his victory as his hand hovered over the shutdown switch that would send the blast doors slamming closed and seal us to our fate.

His hubris was his mistake.

Even as he laughed, a guard walked to the security door, opening it in response to a request from the other side. Through the thick, distorted glass I watched it open, and then a guard strut through with a satisfied grin on his face. Gateau's laughter only faltered when Ezzi, who'd followed the guard from their private rendezvous, picked up a metal stool and smashed it into both guards with vicious swings. He spun as they collapsed into unconscious heaps on the ground, but it was too late. She'd already launched herself at him with a look of such pure hatred that I felt almost sorry for him.

Almost.

When he was unconscious, Ezzi hit the separate buzzers to open first one massive gate, then the next. Then she went right back to beating the toad at her feet, kicking at him repeatedly before picking up a stool and swinging it again and again into his sides and face. We had to beat upon the guardhouse door for her to open it so we could take her with us. She only lost the wild look in her eyes when she realized Rio held her son.

"Thank you," I said simply, Rio handing Mateo to her. She signed the child hello with tears in her eyes. "One of those *bastardos* is his father. But I'll never tell Mateo that. I'll say his father was a prisoner in el Castillo, because I want him to be proud of his *Papa*."

A gun cocked on my left. "This won't take long," Diego muttered, his eyes on the unconscious man with the gold watch just inside the guardhouse gate. "He was going to kill me. I think I'll repay the favor."

I opened my mouth to say something, but Rio beat me to it. His hand snaked out to stay Diego's arm. "There's been enough violence today, Diego. Enough anger. He'll go to hell, but not by our hands."

Diego paused, but then nodded. "As you wish *el Lobo*." He said it like an honorific.

With the prison doors open, the mob rioting in the courtyard were now sprinting for the exit. More and more inmates were streaming into the courtyard from buildings; the short corridor to freedom now packed with fleeing prisoners. Whatever crimes they had committed, their time in el Castillo had absolved them. They'd paid their price, and I wished them luck in their newfound freedom.

We walked slowly down the short passageway to the final gate—Rio, Diego, Ezzi, Mateo and I—and the crowds parted around us. People were running across the expanse of land, disappearing into the markets. When we reached them, Rio stopped.

"Rio, we should go."

"I know. It's just…" Rio turned to me with wonder in his eyes. He shook his head as he stared back at el Castillo.

"I'd given up hope, Bella. Of ever escaping this place. Of beating the system. Of…" he swallowed, and suddenly I was reminded of another time I'd been standing in this place, facing this huge, tattooed man and staring at a castle. "Of ever finding someone like you."

He took my hands and pulled me into him. "I love you so much. Whatever happens, I'll never leave you."

Then he pulled me into a kiss that was born of hope, inspired by love, and made in freedom.

EPILOGUE - BELLA

"Hello Papa! Rio and I have something to tell you."

My father's face beamed back at me from the computer. He'd taken an immediate liking to the man who'd fallen in love with his daughter, and his political contacts had been invaluable in getting him a passport to slip from the country. We were now chatting to him from a small shack on a remote beach in South America, our first contact since we'd left the country several months ago.

"That's wonderful Bella. I have something to tell you too," he said, his eyes excited. "Several things, actually."

"Okay, you first," I said with a grin. I motioned Rio to come and sit beside me. He'd just returned from a swim, and beads of water ran over his copper skin as he toweled himself dry, put on a shirt, and came to sit beside me.

"Well first, you'll be happy to know that el Castillo has been closed—permanently."

Rio's tanned face ran white. "What?" He ran a trembling hand through his still wet hair. "*Señor* Martin, that's wonderful news. I never thought I'd see the day."

"I told you, call me Maurice." My father grinned. "And I thought you would like it. As we discussed the day you left, I've been working on it tirelessly. It's a major win for ethical treatment of prisoners in this country. They have plans to use the structure as housing for the poor."

Rio sobered. "What about the current prisoners?"

"All of the inmates with misdemeanor charges were released, and those with more serious crimes sent on to other prisons," my father said. Then he chuckled. "That being said, there weren't that many people to send on. I don't think the authorities looked too hard for the ones that made it out—not after I blew the whistle on what had been going on, on the inside."

"And Gateau?"

"He's one of those 'serious crimes' I mentioned. He'll be in maximum security for the rest of his life. I hear there are quite a lot of prisoners who want to have a quiet word with him while he's in there."

Rio nodded. "All good things," he said, finally allowing himself to break into a grin. "You've done well, Maurice, that is good news indeed." He looked to me. "Did you tell him yet?" he asked.

I shook my head. "I was about to. Papa-"

Maurice coughed. "Actually, I've got one other piece of news I need to tell you—someone I think you might like to meet." He motioned off camera to someone beside him. "Ezzi, would you like to say hello?"

My hands went to my mouth in a squeal as Ezzi appeared, Mateo in her arms. "Oh my God!" I hadn't seen her since we fled the country. She looked like a new woman.

Ezzi's cheeks were plumper than they'd been the day of our escape—they had a healthy glow that was reflected in her eyes. *She was beautiful.*

Ezzi smiled at me, biting her lip. "Hi Bella, how are you?"

"You look amazing!" I gushed. "Have you… are you clean?"

Even her hair had more life—it bounced when she gave a proud nod. "Your father has been so kind to me, Bella. I don't know how I can ever repay him." She eyed him with a glance that said they'd shared many coffees over the past few months. "Though, I do know how to start."

Papa looked at me sheepishly when I raised an eyebrow. He scratched his thinning hair. "She's, ah… she's making me start dating again. Set me up with an app called *Tinder*."

If I'd had coffee I would have spat it out.

Papa frowned at the look on my face. "Have I done the wrong thing? Is it too soon?"

I chuckled. "Not at all. Just, have fun, okay?" Oh God, this was my father I was talking to. I actually started to blush.

In Ezzi's arms, Mateo waved. "Hi *Tita* Bella. Hi Rio!"

Rio laughed, signing the little child back, but spoke for my benefit as well. "You finally got your battery!"

Mateo nodded, his face super serious. "Yes. Papá Martin and I decided that we should stay here, at the embassy, while the guards are looking for Mama. I help out in the garden to pay our way."

"He's been a great help," my father said, ruffling the little child's hair. "After the riot, I thought they would be safer here, where the local police can't look." He bit his lip, turning serious. "I don't know what I would have done without them, truthfully. It's been so good to have friends around the house." He settled more comfortably on his seat, pulling Mateo over to sit on his lap. "But what about your news. You said you had something to tell me?"

I grinned, and looked to Rio. He took me into a protective cuddle, his own smile getting wider and wider.

"Oh, nothing much," I said, forcing an air of casualness. Then I burst into happy laughter, unable to keep the tears from my eyes. "Just, Mateo's about to get a playmate."

— *The End* —

To join Nikki's VIP reader group and receive three free novellas, go to: www.nightvisionbooks.com/nikki-steele

AUTHOR'S NOTE

Thank you for reading The Beast & the Beauty! It may interest you to know that the characters in this story are fictional, but *el Castillo* is, rather remarkably, based on truth.

In Honduras, the *Danlí* prison houses 700 inmates, has only 240 beds, and just 15 full time guards. The prisoners run wild within its walls. The guards ask for permission from gang leaders before they venture inside.

In Bolivia, *San Pedro* prison is famous for running prison tours through its slums and shanty towns (you just need to bribe the guard at the front gate). The prison was designed to house 600 inmates but now holds 3000. The families of the convicted often live with them in their cells.

In many corrupt South American prisons, crooked guards use the inmates to make cocaine and other drugs.

When I discovered this, the story of two lovers trapped in these conditions entered my head and just wouldn't go away. The result was The Beast & the Beauty, which you've just read. I sincerely hope you enjoyed the story.

If you did enjoy it, you may be interested to know that I'm thinking of writing a second book which revolves around the adventures of Ezzi and her young son. Ezzi had a relatively minor role in The Beast & the Beauty, though she was critically important—Bella and Rio couldn't have escaped without her! She's suffered so much and is such a complex person that I feel she deserves her own Bad Boy fairytale happy ending. I'd love to know what you think.

It would be remiss of me if I didn't make a special shout out in these author's notes to my editor Taryn Ulrich. Writing the first draft of a story is a solitary task, but subsequent edits should not be. Taryn was originally a reader who contacted me because she found spelling errors in one of my already published books. I was so impressed that I asked her to be the editor for this one. She's done an amazing job (seriously, you should have seen this book before she got it!). Taryn, thank you very much.

If you have enjoyed my work and are interested in knowing when Ezzi's tale comes out, please sign up to my newsletter! You'll also get 3 free stories as well. You can do so at www.nightvisionbooks.com/nikki-steele.

Regards, and happy reading.

Nikki

FURTHER READING

I write about strong female characters that are independent and opinionated. I hope you enjoy my books!

You can find all of my books on Amazon at http://Author.to/NikkiSteele. I'd love a review!

You can sign up for my newsletter at www.nightvisionbooks.com/nikki-steele

You can find me on Facebook at www.facebook.com/nikkisteeleauthor

And you can chat to me in person at nikki@nightvisionbooks.com

Made in the USA
Middletown, DE
17 February 2018